My Children
My Teachers

Help Your Children Realize
Their True Potential!

Sandeep Nair

VISHWAKARMA
PUBLICATIONS **VP**

My Children My Teachers

Edition - July 2016
© Author

ISBN - 978-93-83572-67-0

Published by:
Vishwakarma Publications
283, Budhawar Peth, Near City Post,
Pune- 411 002.
Phone No: (020) 20261157
Email: info@vpindia.co.in
Website: www.vpindia.co.in

Cover Design
Abhishek Darekar

Typeset and Layout
Gold Fish Graphics, Pune.

Acknowledgements

Writing this book was by no means one person's journey. It thus gives me immense pleasure to acknowledge the significant contributors who helped me in the composition of the book.

I am indebted to those who walked every step through thick and thin. While this book may bear my name, it would never be printed without the unweary commitment of Asha (my wife), Radhakrishna Pai (friend), Indira Ramachandran (sister in law), Gaurang Bookseller (friend) and Suresh Rane (friend).

I'm humbled by those who took time out of their busy schedule to share their views and in some cases validate my hypothesis. I'm grateful to Dr. Shreeram Geet, Dr. Bhooshan Shukla, Dr. Yajyoti Singh, Ms. Anu Aga, Dr. Anand Patkar, Mr. Nitin Deshpande and Mr. Tanmoy Bandyopadhyay.

Then there are those who not only helped but also believed in me, shared feedback/articles, suggested alternate ideas, helped with contacts etc. I am obliged to Mr. Shyam Sundar Vaidyanathan, Mrs. Tejasvita Apte, Mrs. Mini Sukumaran Nair, Mr. Nandakumar Kandeswarath, Mr. Sandeep Bhat, Mr. Piyush Sharma, Mrs. Meenu Gupta, Dr. Meenakshi Thorat, Mrs. Sobha Jaidev, Mr. Manjinder Singh Nijjar, Mr. Nandakumar Kandammattil, Mr. Bharat Pallod, Mr. Sameer Paralikar, Mr. Ashutosh Saitwal, Mr. Mahesh Narkar and Mr. Hemant Ambikar.

Last but not least, I would like to thank Ms. Scharada Dubey and Vishwakarma Publication for giving me this opportunity, M. Purushoutham for sprucing up my language and Kumari Kumudini Bendre for formulating the lovely cover.

Expert comments from

Dr. Shreeram Geet
B.A.M.S, Career Counselor, Writer and Medical Practitioner

Dr. Geet was the Coordinator & Staff Training In-charge at Sanjeevan Hospital, Pune for 11 years. He is a Founder Secretary of General Practitioner Association, Pune 1991-93. He was in-charge of Career Guidance Cell, Jnana Prabodhini Samshodhan Sanstha, Pune from 1999-2010. He has given career guidance to more than 10,000 students at Jnana Prabodhini, Pune. He has been invited as a guest speaker at various prestigious forums including Directorate of Technical Education, Dhirubhai Ambani Foundation, Mahratta Chambers of Commerce, Indian Medical Association and Daily Sakal; and has given more than 300 lectures all over Maharashtra.

Dr. Bhooshan Shukla
MD (Psychiatry), DNB (Psychiatry), MRC Psych (London), Diploma in Clinical Hypnosis (UK)., Child and Adolescent Psychiatrist

Dr. Bhooshan is a trained Psychiatrist qualified both in India and the UK. He has vast experience dealing with mental health issues of children and families in India and abroad. His special expertise lies in the field of psychotherapy (Cognitive - Behavioral Therapy, Gestalt Therapy, Family Therapy, Parent Training, Hypnosis and Personal Coaching). He is a Europe-certified EMDR Practitioner, a special therapy used on children and adult survivors of traumatic experiences. Dr. Bhooshan has conducted numerous workshops and training programmes for medical and non-medical professionals in this field.

Dr. Yajyoti Singh

B.Ed. in special education, Masters in Developmental Psychology, Ph. D. in Social Sciences with her Dissertations in Developmental Psychology.

Dr. Yajyoti Singh is a Consultant Developmental and Educational Psychologist based in Pune and is the Proprietor and founder member of Chetana Centre for Mental Health. She has been the HOD and Consultant Psychologist with the Bishop's Schools for 14 years. She has over 24 years of experience working with toddlers, children, adolescents and adults with a range of Educational and Developmental issues, including Learning Difficulties, Attention Deficit Disorder, PDD/ Autism and other developmental and behavioral problems, using major tests of general ability, academic attainment, continuous performance tasks and neuropsychological tests. She conducts workshops on Parenting skills, stress management, positive thinking, coping techniques, teacher training, memory improvement techniques, time management, gender sensitivity etc. at various schools and organizations. She has been the consultant psychologist at various hospitals including Ruby Hospital and is currently with Sahayadri Hospitals besides schools and remand homes.

Table of Contents

Introduction

'Children must be taught how to think, not what to think.'

~ **Margaret Mead**

Thank you for choosing to read my book.

Unaware I was that the turning point in my life came with the birth of our first child. Watching her arrive in this world, I got my first lesson, a flashback of the past 32 years of my life revealing to me that for all the pain my parents went through in raising me, I could have been a much better son.

I realized my angel was here to teach me, and be my conscience. Two years later on the very same day of the year, another bundle of joy arrived into our life, and brought along my reflection. With both conscience and reflection pairing up, I have been showered with learning ever since. There is no shame in admitting that my children have helped me understand myself. They have been my inspiration, coach and motivation thus forming the name of my book.

My learning as a parent, coupled with my observations in a managerial capacity at work made me wonder, how I could help my children realize their true potential. The initial stumbling helped me realize that the way to achieve my goal was to look for opportunities in the challenges they threw at me. Often, my best efforts were received with huge resistance making me feel helpless. This feeling of helplessness, which later brought out the best in me, exposed the lack in me of one basic ingredient: empathy. That aside, the countless failures and frustrations are the true witnesses to the pleasures experienced as a parent!

This book is an attempt to fuel the reader's thoughts. The viewpoints presented here are founded based on experience gathered over the years and aimed at understanding children. It is thus dedicated to my little gems, life without whom would have had little meaning. I hope my experiences and viewpoint guides them as they grow to realize their dreams.

Hope you enjoy reading it as much as I enjoyed writing it!

Parenting Legacy

'The only thing you take with you when you're gone is what you leave behind.' ~ John Allston

8:30 AM, 13ᵗʰ of June 2013. I was anxiously waiting for the desk phone to ring. Such a moment had never arrived in the 25 years of my IT career. As Dr. Spencer Johnson had put it, changes are often visible to those who look for it, I had sensed what was coming.

The phone rang and with the usual greetings over, my boss said, "You have probably guessed the reason behind this call." He then appreciated the changes that I had driven over the years. As if to placate, he stated the decision to let me go was organizational and that he had recommended me to other groups. I was keen on ending the call while he walked me through the paper work. I thanked him for the opportunity and the great time we had working together.

No matter how long and hard you work, nothing prepares you for a situation such as this. What hurt me was the fact that I had just got into a rhythm and had in ways rediscovered my true passion. Just a few years ago, I had learnt to differentiate myself and had developed an understanding of what mattered - my values and brand.

This abrupt ending was confusing; I deserved a graceful exit. There was however no point in refuting that all good things come to an end. In some ways, I was fortunate to have a coach; she guided me by being my mirror and helped me realize who I was. She encouraged me to be different and to pursue what I believed in. Every grey cloud they say has a silver lining and may be this incident too would have a meaning and a story to tell.

The drive back home was probably the longest 15 minutes ever. On the one hand, I felt the need for self-pity and on the other the urge to get over it. Aware that once weaned, the only thing that would matter is how gracefully I handled the situation, I hung in there. Reaching home early often got the kids excited. However, things today seemed different. Our pet dog Buddy too seemed to sense my grief, vigorously attempting to lick it off. The children's faces though lacking expressions were soaked in questions while trying to understand the situation. Putting up a brave face, I decided to explain. The elder one, Rashi 15, has a shy and conscious facade. At the core though was a strong willed, talented, independent and an ambitious soul tightly packed in a petite built. She was more curious on how it had happened, didn't I see it coming, was today my last day at work and so on. Rushil, the younger one all of 13 has a stocky outer shell with a presence that is supplemented by a compassionate, creative and hospitable core. He went right for the gut asking if it meant he shall not go to school tomorrow. Oddly, their curiosity seemed to comfort me!

Anita, my better half has always been very supportive. She was calm, having heard the news earlier. Noticing the kids all over me, she reminded them of their homework. By evening, I was composed though I realized it was going to be a long evening. A self-learner of sorts, I believed in savoring such defining moments. As night unfolded, the beers ensured fewer distractions and helped me dig on my achievements. In the background, Jagjit and Chitra Singh were lightening the atmosphere with their mellifluous rendition. Rashi would drop by occasionally to pick on the peanuts while Rushil ensured the mug stayed full to the brim. He enjoyed playing with the froth. By midnight, the songs seemed more meaningful and surroundings lonely. I was starting to feel like a king, proud of my little kingdom. I was a proud father, a reasonable son and not bad a husband.

The ensuing days were unusually dull and clouded with thoughts. I had started visualizing the opportunity enveloped within the incident. The spectrum of thoughts varied from doing a coast-to-coast road trip to the desire to give something back to the community. Often pondering about my calling in life, I wondered if there was one. How did people find theirs, is it always a hindsight? With thoughts competing to grab my mind share, confusion was inevitable.

Dozing on the chair, Rashi's question jolted me to consciousness. Did you share it with your parents? Sharing it over the phone would make them worried. It was preferable instead to do it in person. A week had passed and yet there were no concrete steps ahead. I grabbed my pen and rough book which mostly consisted of interior design sketches and activities for the kids. A pen in hand tends to put my mind into overdrive. Realizing this I reach for one whenever I am grappling with conflicting thoughts. Listing them down I realized they formed a pattern with some being short-term goals and the rest long-term. The short-term ones as the name suggests, were immediate needs more like a wish-list reflecting recreational and other needs while the long-term to-do list reflected career-related things, which could wait.

I met Anita in the kitchen to explore ways to make the short term wish list a reality. Convincing her on the opportunity of doing a coast-to-coast road trip felt premeditated like one of those moments, where how-so-ever obvious it may be, you want the other person to decide and own your guilt. When schools are in session, so is Anita. Even going bird-watching would require me to join a group. Being the kind who enjoyed family comfort, doing a trip without them would seem boring and meaningless. With every item on the short-term list requiring breaks, the list got wiped-out in no time. Dejected, I was in no mood to think of the long-term ones.

Weekend approaching it was time to give the short-term list another try. One of the things I enjoyed most was washing the car. It was not about the looks or the workout but the tranquility it brought me. I considered this my personal time and enjoyed going into deep thought while at it. Approaching the list a little differently I probed, 'What if, I were to be run over by a truck?' Surprisingly, after a brief moment of thought, none of the item on the list mattered! What mattered was making Rushil independent with regards to his education. Suddenly out of nowhere, I knew my priorities and there were no second thoughts. It kind of bothered me that the most important item did not figure in either of the list. I however felt glad for not having missed it.

Anita and I had an agreement on how to deal with our children's education. She focused on their daily activities and I on their long term goals. The latter mostly consisted of programs, such as giving impromptu speeches, watching educational videos, realizing areas of strength and those requiring improvement, learning to prioritize, improvising grades, etc. Excited and eager to share my findings with her, I did not bother to think it through. I cautiously approached her with the thought of taking over Rushil's education, explaining how such an arrangement would also let me work closely to understand him better. Her silence seemed louder than the continuous humming of the ceiling fan! To avoid her feeling targeted, I kept going. This is not about you it is about Rushil, I told her. Often while doing the same thing repetitively we tend to look at things minutely while missing out on the larger picture. Our approaches being different could help complement our understanding of him. In addition, it would also give us a much-needed break. She responded, "For how long can you commit yourself to this responsibility? You do realize this is not a short-term task." I admitted to taking at least six months to achieve something meaningful and I would know more once my long-term plans were figured out. Her agreement, albeit unconvinced was voiced as "we need to cut down on our expenses".

With obvious hesitation, I approached Rushil explaining how and why he was on top of my list of priorities. Intent on helping, I described how another pair of eyes could help view things differently. Anita and I agreed that he was putting in more study time than required and the goal would be to extract more playtime. On the surface, he seemed more worried about me not going to work than me coaching him. Probably our different styles were playing on his mind. She was strict but helpful and Rushil was comfortable with her style. I was lenient and the guiding kind, which often resulted in more work. To persuade him further, I apprised him of her consent and he agreed. Observing and figuring out the changes would need a few weeks. We thus agreed to continue as usual during which time his mom would be available for assistance.

My decision to work with Rushil brought with it a sense of satisfaction that was not easy explaining to the elders. How could the bread winner of the family decide to stay home and that too with kids so young? Who could be stupid enough to give up such a high paying career? Isn't Anita already taking care of the children's education? All the ranting seemed to chip at my conviction. As days passed, with kids at school, morning hours were getting increasingly unproductive. One of the items on my to-do list was to document the activities I had conducted with them over the years with the objective of helping them understand the rationale behind them. Just documenting though did not seem fulfilling enough. I wanted to do more. My sister-in-law, Mandira fueled these thoughts further, persuading me that it could be a good read for other parents. She had always been curious of the activities I conducted. The idea of publishing it though was not comforting as never in my dreams did I take myself to be a writer. The only things I had ever written were technical documents. Though uneasy, the thought of sharing my experiences did seem difficult to put down. It aligned perfectly with my motto of "Making a difference by investing in people" and one of my cherished values of leaving behind a legacy. Thus, the idea of writing a book was here to stay. The word quickly spread amongst the children, their cousins and to everyone in the previous generation. I was once again in the crosshair for trying to do something different.

It meant a lot of learning and unlearning, starting from scratch and rebuilding. It reminded me of my ex-boss, who advised fidgeting with one parameter at a time. Here I was experimenting with something that was entirely new. For starters, I had no background in child psychology nor was I accustomed to writing and neither did I have a good command over the language. To make things worse, I was a selective reader and read books that were either management or career related. In all, there were a ton of downsides and only one upside, my passion to make a difference.

Rashi loves scribbling in my rough book, as if to mark her territory. I caught her scribbling and to divert my attention, she asked 'What was the point in writing your wish list, when the final outcome was something very different?' I responded by telling her that though it may look like a throw-away exercise, it is not as it helps organize and prepare ones mind to yield better understanding and thoughts. Going through the drill, gives me the satisfaction of having made the right choice. How one works towards evolving ones' thoughts is immaterial as long as they know the method that works for them.

Getting started on the book required answering a bunch of questions like how do I stitch them into a story, what problems would the book help address, how would the book differentiate itself, who would be the targeted audience, etc. Questions greatly outnumbered the answers and while being pertinent and imperative, started to drain me. In parallel Rashi and Rushil helped compile the activities I had conducted with them over the years. Elaborating these prompted me to think of the reasons behind them. Was it because I had read it somewhere or did I hear it from other parents? Having drawn a blank, I asked Anita if she recollected. She mentioned, it was something about people facing challenges at work and whenever opportunity surfaced, I thought of an activity. As I pondered further, two reasons became prominent; one, my observations at the work place and the other, the "legacy" I so passionately wanted to leave behind.

My ideas were further honed when we met Anita's uncle Mr. Balvanth, a successful entrepreneur running a small-scale business. On becoming aware of my plans to write and that too on parenting, his questions were: why in the world you and how does IT and Parenting share any commonality or even a vague relation? I was pressured into explaining.

I blurted out that while in a management role, I noticed quite a few talented and educated people struggling to be effective after just a few years of service."

Startled by my explanation, he asked, "What do you mean? Doesn't a degree from a reputed university and a 7-digit salary imply effectiveness?"

I explained further "Smart people though they are, they face difficulty in gauging where their careers are headed. Earning well they do but with little idea of where they want to be 5 to 10 years down the line and most importantly, why. They seem to lack a sense of direction and an understanding of what matters. Those who do face a different kind of challenge- overcoming hurdles that the corporate world puts before them."

Uncle interjected, "What hurdles?"

"Hurdles such as dealing with change, working as a team, having a sense of ownership, accepting criticism, etc."

Uncle remarked, "Are they unable to do their jobs or are they in the wrong jobs."

I said, "No, it is not about doing their jobs; instead, it is about being able to make a difference at what they do. Those aware of the change they want are driven and stop at nothing."

Uncle's cornering was actually helping me connect the dots.

Unconvinced yet curious, Uncle shot off further questions. "Assuming people have difficulty in being effective and realizing their true potential, what has that got to do with parenting?"

Pardoning the long answer, I said. "Parenting has evolved over generations and has been reflective of the era that children were born in. In the times of joint families, the emphasis of parenting was on shared responsibilities and so was ownership. There was little room for individuality or individual priorities. Separate sources of income gave rise to the concept of individual priorities and thus came about nuclear families. This brought along further change in the meaning of parenting. Parents were now responsible for everything including education and establishing children. The latter's instinct thus adapted to the changes taking place around them, learning from surrounding, peer parents, books etc."

"This also created a rift in social order especially in those with conscious parenting instinct. They felt the need to explore, be different and thus became the trendsetters. Their findings spread and thus grabbed other parent's attention. It is this instinct that has helped parents raise children successfully over generations. Acknowledging the challenges that we observe with the youth, and leveraging them as opportunities within parenting will help in finding solutions, and thus addressing them in the future. Parenting will continue to evolve; the next wave would include looking beyond. "

Uncle confirmed, "Do you mean the emphasis from here on will be on the how?"

I said, "Rightly, the future generation of parents will focus on depth and the quality of parenting. The focus will not just be on raising children successfully but also to make them aware of themselves".

Uncle remarked, "Why is it that other people do not notice this need for change?"

In explanation I said, "My exposure to the work-place and its dynamics afforded me with a top - down view. These cues from the corporate world if inculcated into our parenting practices, we can effectively influence parenting legacy and bring about a difference in the way future generations are reared thus augmenting the legacy that passes from one generation to the next."

A week later, I met my ex-boss over dinner and while apprising him of the situation was asked with curiosity of how the "parenting legacy" was coming along. Couple of minutes into my explanation, he prompted and requested that I summarize the takeaways in three brief sentences. My feeble attempts were giving me away and I decided to return with an answer. While my Boss liked the problem statement, he expected the takeaways to be crisper. It thus brought in the realization that crispier takeaways would help with the flow of the book.

Understanding the takeaways required multiple passes starting with challenges that people face in the work place. Next, these challenges were grouped together based on associating attributes which were nothing but answers to issues such as the mapping of a child's behavior, the challenge this experiment would help overcome, who does it involve, the child, parent or both, etc. The groupings helped me arrive at specific themes and thus concoct a story.

When you enjoy what you do, time passes by unnoticed. It was April - a full 10 months from the time I took up the book. An entire academic year had ended with schools closing for summer vacations. My 300-page foolscap book was full of notes with my book in its third draft. Calls from headhunters had started to dry up.

While the initial themes made sense, in subsequent previews, parents found it difficult to connect with. Plans were off target by miles though the scope for learning was immense and most importantly, I continued to grow as a parent. Though the book was a long way from completion, it was already making a difference in my life- My desire to leave a parenting legacy was growing stronger and my viewpoints starting to resonate with friends and reviewers. The book was finally down to three parts.

Watching Ones Actions

Watch your thoughts; they become words. Watch your words; they become actions. Watch your actions; they become habit. Watch your habits; they become character. Watch your character; it becomes your destiny.' ~ **Lao Tzu**

One late evening, Rashi was awake past her bedtime. She was not too happy with how I had conducted myself after being apprised of Rushil's stealing money. His music instructor at school had recommended buying a Yamaha Flute. She opined that my earlier decision to decline his request for a flute left him with no choice but to steal. She felt that his music instructor and I were pulling him apart. None of us were willing to understand his situation and given that, his actions seemed justified. This discussion coming from an 11 year old pacified my rage and left me speechless. She seemed to outgrow her age!

I kept pondering on how she could see through my inappropriate behavior, while I could not. Is it that hard to see one's action? As a professional, I believed in actions more than words though it never seemed to transcend into family life. Cautious of being watched, the thought of punishment reminded me of what I had learnt from my pet dog Kalu, a mongrel resembling a shepherd dog. During my teenage days, Kalu often tricked my mom and ran through the front door. He was ferocious, and would create a ruckus on the street. The most embarrassing of all, would be his rolling over rotten garbage. Worried that he might invite trouble, either my brother or me would launch a hunt to get him back. Excited by our sight, he would run further away. The only way to get hold of him was to ambush him. Once caught, I would often vent my frustration by pounding him. One evening, after the incident I wondered what prevented Kalu from coming to me, especially when he was excited to see me. Was it because I would take him back home or was it because he knew, I would pound him? That incident made me realize, why Kalu or for that matter anybody would not want to be caught for a wrong doing especially when they are aware of the treatment. Keeping this teaching in mind, I went soft on Rushil's punishment and made him rehearse the flute, 15 minutes every day for the next month.

The questions, 'How could my actions be consistent with my beliefs?' and 'How could I learn to watch my actions?' loomed large.

Learn Teach Learn

*'In learning you will teach, and in teaching you will learn'- **Phil Collins***

Parenting as I experienced is an ongoing process of building and reinforcing. Techniques learnt either from books or peers hardly fit. Just when you feel settled, the child grows up and throws another set of surprises. The arrival of the sibling is welcomed with a familiarity that does not linger for long. Applying the learning onto the younger one yields little but frustration. They cry out loud expressing their individuality and yet we stayed submerged, comparing and worrying about every little aspect from speaking their first word to potty training. Only when you learn to unlearn, understand their different needs and treat them accordingly, do they realize the benefits of similar treatment.

Now how do you treat them differently and yet maintain parity?

I like to describe it as a process of continuous learning; learning from children, revising and teaching it back to them and repeating it all over again. What made it interesting was my preference for the path of resistance, most resistance as opposed to least. They made me revisit my childhood, learn about myself as an individual, question my methods and ensure consistencies. It seemed to remind me of a mirror in that children are more than a reflection of their parents when approached with an open mind. Doing so, they can be excellent teachers. Here are some areas that afforded me good learning.

Unraveling Oneself

'Knowing others is intelligence; knowing yourself is true wisdom.' ~ **Lao Tzu**

It was early in the November of 2010 that I delivered a speech at my father's funeral which left me reflecting upon myself. For some reason, I spoke of him as an individual and not as my father. What stood out about him was not the father in him or the husband; it was him as a person- honest, non-judgmental and helpful. I kept wondering why his qualities as an individual mattered more than as a parent. Never before did I feel the urge to appreciate him and share what he meant to me. He probably was well aware of not being the best dad, but he ought to know that he did a lot of things right. I continued wondering if he had spent any time reflecting on what his children thought about him, and would knowing his children's feelings surprise him?

As a professional, I have spent reasonable time reflecting on goals, performance, behavior etc. However, as a parent the emphasis was always on my children. In some ways, I was obsessed with continuing the legacy of making the next generation more successful. I would actively seek challenges, ensure their days were productive and vacations meaningful. Whether it was staying physically active or having personal goals, I had most of it covered. The activities I picked were neither random nor lacking in direction. Every activity brought along expectation that kept mounting. It was as if my parenting approach was driven more by the anxiety of proving my parenting prowess.

Looking back, one of the positive takeaways from my father's demise was realizing the need to step back and slow down. I was a parent on the express-highway of life wanting everything for my most priced assets. I clearly lacked understanding of the things that mattered the most be it education or happiness or disciplining them or encouraging them to be themselves. It all pointed toward one thing: the need to understand myself as a parent.

Dr. Shreeram Geet - Its common for parents to expect their child to succeed where they have failed. For all the mistakes one makes, parents expect to compensate that in their child. Parents, who retrospect are unlikely, to burden children with their expectation and use them to fulfill their unfulfilled dreams.

It was not easy reconciling the fact that in all the activities that I pushed my children into carried some level of expectation. Irrespective of the situation, my pride was always at stake. Whether it was their performance in school or their behavior in the presence of guests, I had difficulty accepting my children as being normal. I kept pushing for more.

Even after realizing the need to understand one's self as a parent, I was clueless on its approach. At first, the whole concept sounded exciting but putting the pieces together became an overwhelming exercise. The thoughts lacked structure and the message was hardly persuasive. Fortunately, convincing others involved in the exercise was a blessing in disguise as the constant confrontation forced me to articulate things better.

Knowing oneself as a parent can be broadly summed into three aspect a) Knowing ones beliefs, priorities and expectation, b) Being aware of one's parenting styles and, c) Being aware of similarities in traits.

Dr. Yajyoti Singh - Knowing oneself is about being consistent as a parent. Being consistent implies knowing ones beliefs, priorities, expectations, goals etc. Parents, incognizant of themselves are bound to have difficulty being the pillar or support for the child. Parents who struggle to know simple things, such as their priority are bound to confuse children with their additional baggage.

I had already learnt of my handicaps of growing expectations. What started as simple prayers for a healthy child seemed to get compounded with every passing year. Whether it was about swimming or reading non-fictional books, the focus was always on expectation. It was starting to become awfully clear that I had no clue what I really expected from my children. When viewed from a child's perspective the messaging could easily be construed as not being good at anything.

As for my priorities, they too didn't seem sorted-out either. My claim of the children's welfare being my top priority was not in sync with the time I spent with them or the degree of my involvement with their upbringing. I was more of a weekend parent. Being just the provider was not adding up.

While I believed in being consistent with my beliefs, I never attempted to write down and live by them. Whenever situations were favorable, I never failed to live my beliefs. On all other occasions, I backed it up with sound reasoning. Children often saw beyond the gaps, they learnt that no matter what, you do back it up with sound justification!

Dr. Bhooshan Shukla - Beliefs are very conscious things developed over time. People when asked about their beliefs give a rosy picture of what they would like to believe, not actually what they believe in. In psychology, we say beliefs are irrelevant, actions are what count.

The second aspect that helped me know myself was my parenting style. While most people disagree on the term, it helps group the different behaviors parents tend to exhibit. In hindsight, I could easily be classified as being caring, over protective, experimenting, having too much expectation and not very supportive a parent. Our individual nature seems to be at play here with some having difficulty trusting while there are others who trust blindly. There are those who believe in helping and there are others who choose to coach. Some are forgiving while others penalize. We carry forward what we admire and refrain from those that we detest. Nurturing what we value, an honest parent is likely to nurture the same in their child. A pessimistic parent is bound to confine their child's freedom, whereas an ambitious parent is bound to stretch their child.

Dr. Bhooshan Shukla - Parent need to realize they have a choice. They do not have to go down the same path again and again. An anxious parent is likely to fall back on strategies that are part of their experiences growing up. Parents who step back, realize nothing is at stake and exercise their choice are less likely to follow the path of least resistance i.e. what's already hardwired up there.

Since my parenting practices were tuned to suit the individual child's needs, they often varied between children. I can recount instances of being unfair to our elder child. We often expected her to be mature, well behaved, grow beyond her age and be the role model for the younger sibling. This got to a point where the younger one aware of his leeway, exploited it to the hilt. The elder one, noticing the free rein started leveraging him to meet her demands as well. Noticing patterns only after situations blew out of proportion helped in re-emphasizing the need to know our parenting style. While there is no such thing as a right or a wrong style, building an understanding of one's style can bring in awareness and help stay consistent.

Parenting Style is a combination of parental control and parental responsiveness ([1]Elizabeth Nixon and Ann Marie Halpenny). Parental control refers to the demands that parents place upon their children to be mature and responsible individuals, and the rules and limits that parents set and enforce for their children. Parental responsiveness refers to the degree of support, warmth and affection that parents display towards their children.

Two Dimensional classification of Parenting Styles

		Parental Acceptance/Responsiveness	
		Accepting, Responsive	Rejecting, Unresponsive
Parental Control	Demanding, Controlling	Authoritative	Authoritarian
	Undemanding, Low in control	Permissive-indulgent	Permissive-neglectful

Source: Maccoby and Martin (1983)

---

[1]Elizabeth Nixon and Ann Marie Halpenny, "Perspectives on Parenting Styles and Discipline", http://www.dcya.gov.ie/

The **authoritative** parenting style is represented by high levels of control and maturity demands, in the context of nurturance and open communication. Discipline usually involves the use of reason and power, but not to the extent that the child's autonomy is severely restricted.

The **authoritarian** parenting style, in contrast is identified by high levels of control and demands of the child, coupled with low levels of nurturance. Authoritarian parents engage in low levels of communication with their children, rarely explaining why compliance is necessary. These parents often engage in strong punitive tactics whenever children deviate from their standards (Baumrind, 1967 and 1968).

The **permissive-indulgent** parenting style is characterized by high levels of nurturance and warmth, and low levels of control and maturity demands. This parenting style could be described as an accepting, but lax style of parenting – parents rarely exert control over their children's behavior and do not closely monitor their activities.

The **permissive-neglectful** parenting style is identified by low control and low responsiveness. This style has often been termed 'uninvolved parenting' (Maccoby and Martin, 1983; Teti and Candelaria, 2002).

Dr. Shreeram Geet - Every parent has a different parenting style, something that is not easily defined. Whatever style one practices, the over arching need is to be supportive. Irrespective of the strains, stages and disputes that children and parent go through, if there is support the child stays with the family.

The third aspect and probably the one most noticeable, is the genetic heritage. Right from birth, we take great pride in identifying similarities be it facial features or behavioral characteristics. These rarely go unnoticed. While most of my friends noticed similarities such as flair for languages, photographic memory, hand eye coordination etc., what I noticed was something different. I noticed Rushil at twelve was struggling to cope in school and the pattern looked identical to what I had experienced as a child. While he enjoyed going to school, his notebooks were never complete with a lot of unanswered questions, as if indicating towards an attention deficit. This in some ways urged me to understand my own childhood. It was like digging into an old grave looking for wounds left unattended.

As a child I was physical, the kind who got distracted easily, never caring for consequences. I preferred walking the dog over watching the Sunday evening movie. Compassionate enough to steal, I was strong in regards to trust and integrity and would often confront close friends about their sisters being cheated by other common friends.

Attempting to understand each of the behaviors I exhibited would make for a tedious exercise; instead, I choose to focus on the key ones. It wasn't difficult noticing that I was easily distracted. I would have difficulty assuming things and would often be pre-occupied thinking laterally, trying to connect the dots or looking for alternative approaches.

While on the surface the symptoms may look similar, the root causes might vary significantly. The central idea though was the building of awareness. It certainly brought a difference in my parenting style. My child's creative appetite along with an increased emotional connect made me approach things differently.

Dr. Shreeram Geet - Genetically there are three definite things that gets passed from one generation to the next. The first is intelligence; next motor skills or muscular coordination and third voice coordination. A good surgeon, lawyer, scientist etc. are quite likely to pass on that sort of intelligence to their offspring. As for motor skills, things such as hand eye coordination gets passed down. A sports person's child is very likely to show similar traits as the parent not necessarily in the same sport. There is an old saying, "A singer's child cries in melody".

Though genetic heritages are mostly welcome, factors such as surroundings, education and experiences also contribute towards the individual's development. Owing to such influential factors, it's quite likely that children for varied reasons may not exhibit the same skills as their parent.

Being better equipped to understand myself, I wanted to ensure that I had the best parenting style. I got down to making amendments after amendments leading to one confused parent. Suspecting consequences and worrying about the simplest of things, discussions often ended in quarrels be it with my better-half, parents or my in-laws. I was attempting to bring about a change in everybody and seemed to be in no mood to spare any wrong doer!

With time, I calmed down upon realizing that there was no such thing as a right or wrong style. The key to exploring one's own style lay in understanding the same in all honesty and accepting it. Despite my best efforts, gaps existed in my beliefs and actions that went away with time.

Dr. Bhooshan Shukla - Being authentic is at the core of being a good parent. You cannot be authentic without knowing yourself because you really cannot be what you are not for which you need to know what you are. When it comes to being consistent, parents are actually so in their action. The inconsistencies often lie between their beliefs and their actions.

Looking back on my belief in giving space and freedom to my children, I realize my actions were quite different. I preferred being involved in every decision they made, insisted on knowing all aspects of their life leaving them with little or no privacy. They took me to be a control freak, something that was enough to create friction. This deviance in beliefs and actions became difficult to identify until I learnt about retrospection.

The process of regularly scrutinizing ones actions to reinforce the understanding of the self is called retrospection. Pairing my understanding of parenting styles, beliefs, priorities, expectations, I compiled a list of instances such as decisions made, children's requests, discussion leading up to quarrel(s), unhappiness with self, etc. I further refined the list by prioritizing the ones that needed scrutiny. Digging into each, I started scanning for behaviors and patterns started to emerge. While some were inline with my beliefs there were those that deviated. The deviations are what helped in identifying gaps. Once aware of the deviation, I became more cautious thus helping be myself.

With a baseline in place, the follow-up exercises that came later, were not tedious as they could be done internally in ones' mind. Also, it helped being transparent with Anita and the children by letting them know of my style and beliefs. I remember Anita highlighting a deviation in my style of affording the children exposure and experiences. Having lived overseas, I was somewhat of a hygiene freak. This streak curtailed the children's eating and commuting options. Things such as enjoying street food and travelling by train were never an option. Hinted by Anita and some reflection on my part made me realize how my actions were limiting the children's experiences. Inadvertently, I was pushing my personal experiences on the children not realizing that this behavior was in turn creating barriers and limiting their experiences. By curtailing their exposure, I was taking away an important ingredient in their upbringing i.e. being aware of the surrounding.

Parenting was my utmost responsibility and I was resentful when people learnt things about my children before I did. It was the one thing I proclaimed doing well and how dare anybody raise a finger! When pride was at stake, it did not matter whether the recommendations came from my parents, in-laws or siblings. They were outright rejected. I was missing the point and discouraging all those who wished my children well and wanted them to succeed.

Unraveling one's self took time as the pieces had to fall in place. It is less about winning or losing and more about learning. Given each person's uniqueness, parenting styles are bound to differ. Knowing oneself is not just about developing awareness of one's priorities and expectation but also about ones parenting style and similarities of traits with the children. I am thankfully for being the exploring kind else such genetic heritage would be nothing but hindsight experiences. The biggest value it offers is a view of what the children could be experiencing. The most crucial lesson that I learnt was that there is no such thing as a perfect parent and betterment is a natural process.

Acceptance

'Happiness can only exist in acceptance.' *~***George Orwell**

I am surely not alone in wanting the best for one's children. I didn't expect a lot, just that they harbor the right beliefs, be obedient, stay healthy and positive, be educated enough to make a social impact, live luxuriously, raise a good family and a few others I cannot recollect. A curious friend who was in the know asked "Did the list include Anita's expectation?". Completely missing the underlying sarcasm, I responded quite naively, "no way, she might have hers". He followed up, "how many of your parents' expectation did you live up to?" I abruptly said almost all only to rectify shortly that it could be just two or three. Keen to justify my stand, I relied on the fact that situations were not the same back then and that I was too busy establishing myself. Justification over, the silence was uneasy to the point of annoyance. It was hard, believing I expected too much. Though the goal was to derive more from the child, the means seemed incorrect.

"Each one of us has an internal image of the child that directs us as we begin to relate to a child. This image within prompts us to behave in certain ways; it orients us as we talk to the child, listen to the child, observe the child." [2]Loris Malaguzzi

I too had a built-in image of a child, an image that was superior to me in every aspect. An image, that spoke not just about the child but also the parent. It was something that I had nurtured over the years, a perfect blend of talent, knowledge and skill.

Dr. Shreeram Geet - Acceptance is a must, right from childhood. Though difficult, parents should adopt the policy, 'No Matter What, You Are My Child'. Non-Acceptance seeds comparison and this usually starts with siblings. Kids are often uninterested in what parents wish from them, and parents are rarely informed of child's interests.

---

[2]Loris Malaguzzi, "Your Image of the Child: Where Teaching Begins", https://reggioalliance. org/downloads/malaguzzi:ccie:1994.pdf (collected 10th Nov 2015)

It was starting to become evident that the leading cause of my un-acceptance was the inclination to compare, a clear indicator of my inability to accept things the way they were. Comparisons that are done in parts are nothing but futile, just like the divide and conquer policy that has been exploited successfully for centuries. Given a person's uniqueness, comparing in parts always favors the other, those who are superior in that area. Such tailored comparisons only identify imperfections and un-acceptance. One could be educated and yet disappointed for not being rich. One could be rich and disappointed for not being educated. Any comparisons would make sense only when done as a whole, which unfortunately doesn't seem plausible.

Lack of acceptance seems to lie at the core of who I was as an individual. Having formed roots early on, it grew with me first as a child, then as an adult and continued till parenthood. I was unsure if my inability to accept myself was primary to being accepted by others. I had a lot going for me, be it financial stability, a healthy family or a reasonably successful career. Yet, I was discontent. Every other person seemed to have something I lacked, be it at work or in personal life. I had become adept at comparing and these comparisons supported my lack of acceptance.

Oblivious of the demon inside me, I extended the sphere of comparison to our children as well. Whether it was keeping distraction at bay or being thrifty, I could draw comparisons. It became a tool of convenience helping compare siblings thus pitting one against the other.

My elder daughter Rashi was not the submissive kind. Her continuous retaliation for differential treatment made me realize the individuality in them. As individuals, they were different and gifted in their own way. Their uniqueness was their true strength and my acceptance of it was the first step towards realizing it. Unfortunately, blinded by the thought of deriving the best, I focused only on their shortcomings. It was true that not being in terms with myself (who I was and what I had to offer), I had slim chances of being in good terms with my children.

Dr. Bhooshan Shukla - Comparison is both a necessary and un-necessary evil. Something as simple as sibling rivalry is our very early experience of competition. Most often, we are not looking to scale Mt. Everest. All we want is to do better than our closest competitor. This necessary evil over time spread to all aspects of life, becoming the prime cause of non-acceptance.

"Acceptance is like the fertile soil that permits a tiny seed to develop into the lovely flower it is capable of becoming. The soil only enables the seed to become the flower. It releases the capacity of the seed to grow, but the capacity is entirely within the seed. As with the seed, a child contains entirely within his organism the capacity to develop. Acceptance is like the soil-it merely enables the child to actualize his potential." [3]Dr. Thomas Gordon

"Why is parental acceptance such a significant positive influence on the child? This is not generally understood by parents. Most people have been brought up to believe that if you accept a child he will remain just the way he is; that the best way to help a child become something better in the future is to tell him what you don't accept about him now." [3]Dr. Thomas Gordon

"Therefore, most parents rely heavily on the language of un-acceptance in rearing children, believing this is the best way to help them. The soil that most parents provide for their children's growth is heavy with evaluation, judgment, criticism, preaching, moralizing, admonishing, and commanding-messages that convey un-acceptance of the child as he is." [3] Dr. Thomas Gordon.

Acceptance, unlike any other topic discussed has a multiplier effect. It is not just about parents accepting themselves and their children. It also comprises of children accepting themselves and their parent.

As a child, I often felt targeted, whether at school or at home. I recollect going through a phase where I surmised that a meeting between my parents and my friends was best avoided. It was not my parents' social status or intellectual ability that prevented me from boasting about them. Instead, it was their inability to accept me. What compounded this was my undue comparison of my parents with those of my friends'. I am glad that with time I was able to

---

[3]Dr. Thomas Gordon, "The Power of The Language of Acceptance", http:// http://www. gordontraining.com/ (collected 3 Dec 2015)

be the source of pride that swelled their hearts and hope my children do not continue the unfortunate legacy of my youth.

In hindsight, one realizes that children comparing parents seem as baseless as parents comparing children though it seems to be a recurring theme in most lives. Whether it is getting a mobile phone or vacation to a foreign land, children are equally good at comparing parents. Though superficial, these are often employed to get their wishes fulfilled. Better still, comparison between parents with lines like 'Mommy does not do it that way'! These necessary squabbles have taught both me and my children a lot about each other. They have slowly learnt to see their parent's uniqueness.

Just when I felt cheerful having nipped off an unacceptable habit in the bud, there seemed more! Attempting to draw from my experiences, I often narrated my childhood struggles. This time it was to make them realize the value for money. Recounting my college days when in order to save up for the non-existent pocket money, I would walk 30 minutes to the train station and back. This helped me save the bus fare of 1 Rupee every day. Just when I was almost through, Rushil asked, 'Dad, if you are done with your fairy tales, can I go and finish my homework?'. While upset and offended, I controlled my anger and decided to act unperturbed. As I kept thinking and discussing it with Anita, she reassuringly asked me "Does this too fall under comparison"? Denying at first, I realized that comparing situation or experiences was in many ways analogous to comparing in parts. Further probing made me realize that while my children were keen on hearing about my hardships, what annoyed them was the thing that followed in the form of undue comparisons. The previous generation may have without doubt gone through more hardships than the subsequent lot but one has to take into account changes in the scenario overall. Without accounting for that the entire exercise could be futile.

Dr. Shreeram Geet - Children engaged in finding their niche may often seem distracted, whether it is their deep interests in sport or cultivating hobbies. Lack of understanding and support from parents can easily turn them into drifters.

It was difficult walking the thin line with recently-acquired knowledge on acceptance on the one hand and a desire to make children the best on the other. While focusing on acceptance, I realized the need to not stretch it too far and confuse it with ongoing improvement (s). Accepting did not imply that I stop looking for improvement (s). I drew analogies with diamonds to convince Anita. Raw and precious, they need polishing to help realize their true value. Children are just the same; it is difficult to bring in refinement without improvement. Improvement according to me, does not mean changing the person, instead it should mean broadening one's horizon. Anita would occasionally caution me from getting over-ambitious and recounted an incident of a friend who had difficulty accepting the school's recommendation of detaining their child in the current grade. Instead of accepting the situation and realizing the child's abilities, they committed to making promises on behalf of the child. It is true that losing a year and lagging behind peers may not be the kind of encouragement children need but on the other hand, would more burdens help an already struggling child? Attaching strings such as parents pride and ego can distance the child from being accepted, leaving parents in denial.

The hard truth is comparisons either of individuals, situations or experiences are all recipes for disaster. There is only one way to view things: that of it as a whole. Acceptance with its multiplier effect is not just about parents accepting themselves and their children. It is equally about children accepting themselves and their parents.

Demystifying the Child

'Every person is an unrepeatable miracle.' ~ **Kevin Hall**

A couple of years ago I came in for a surprise, when during a casual chat with peers, I noticed that none were comfortable owning up what their children would become in life. I seemed like an outsider. Perplexed by my own confidence, it took me a while rationalizing the reasons behind my confidence.

Most experts claim parents have little control in what their children will become later in life. Their valuable contribution being support and encouragement, I often felt there was more that parents could do. Looking for cues, I turned to myself. The biggest revelation came about when I started understanding myself, i.e. my individual recipe. A somewhat similar construct I believe holds the key to understanding children.

Understanding children is not about knowing their preferences or likings. It is instead about understanding the ingredients of their unique recipe that helps differentiate an individual from the rest. Like a culinary recipe, an individual's recipe too may consist of instructions and ingredients. While instructions are ones' learning and experiences, ingredients are analogous to individual characteristics. This "recipe" exists for every individual, whether one has experienced it or not.

Like flowers so too every child shall bloom with their individual beauty brought upon by the awareness of their unique recipe. This awareness will also hold the key to positioning oneself in every aspect of life. Where the individual struggles to identify his/ her uniqueness, what then could be the likelyhood of the mass of humanity differentiating the individual?

Dr. Bhooshan Shukla - Realizing what we are good at and for the story to come together takes time. If you look for it, you cannot miss it. Most people are likely to realize their story in their late 30 or 40's. The realization is about being comfortable with their self and not about expecting something spectacular. Those with exceptional biological talent either in music, sport or physical activity may make it big before their twenties. Regardless, it is important to keep those portals open until the moment arrives.

At first, I too couldn't make much between knowing and understanding. The differences, I realized had to be explored. Crudely put, things visible on the surface such as ones' preferred choice of food, clothes, general likes and dislikes, daily routine etc., do help in knowing the child though they reveal precious little when compiled. Additionally, these are subject to frequent changes. These while good to know, are unlikely to help the child's future in any material way.

Understanding the child on the other hand, requires deeper inspection, beyond the obvious and looking for practices and habits that help chart a pattern. These patterns can be noticed in any aspects of development such as physical, mental, emotional or social. Behaviors, which ride these patterns thus reveal the ingredients of the child's recipe. In other words, these behaviors are our window to what the child experiences.

Dr. Yajyoti Singh - It takes time for one to realize their individual blueprint or their child's blueprint. While some attitudes may be dynamic, the core of who we are generally remains constant. Having grown-up children take this up as an exercise can help them visualize getting bolder, communicative, optimistic etc. In addition to introducing them to introspection, it can also give a sense of direction.

Looking for behavioral patterns in activities the child performs all day long quickly became daunting. Instead, I chose to focus on specific set of activities identifying patterns therein. Activities were anything from working on projects, completing worksheets, preparing for a competition or studying for exams. Considering each of these activities as opportunity to learn about the child, I started noting observations. To my surprise, the observations started revealing patterns and potential ingredients of the child's recipe earlier than expected!

Here is an example of some observations captured while a child Nirav, was doing a school project.

- Nirav was engrossed with no distraction of any kind
- Though a group project, he was doing it all alone
- He had to redo the project quite a few times
- During the project, he never asked for help
- In the end, he was able to complete the project just in time

As parents, we can derive multiple outcomes from the observations listed above starting with the fact that Nirav enjoys doing projects and is independent. He is not afraid of mistakes but could do better by involving peers. Though a little unplanned, he does manage to finish it in time. These are all behaviors exhibited by Nirav while performing the activity. When one observes Nirav exhibiting the same behavior repeatedly in other areas as well, what comes forth is a pattern. Such patterns help identify specific behavior that form the ingredient of Nirav's recipe. If Nirav enjoys working on projects most of the time, then 'Enjoys project' is essentially an ingredient of his recipe. If you notice him not involving peers repeatedly, then 'not being a team player' may make another ingredient. Since behavior could very well be situational, it is important to look for consistency before concluding. An individual recipe can consist of both good and not so good ingredients. While the good ingredients are often a child's strength, the not-so-good ingredients bring awareness and could be things that require closer inspection.

Identifying the ingredients of a child's recipe is surprisingly uncomplicated though it requires practice and does not have to be structured as explained earlier. It is an ongoing process of nurturing, refining and adding new ingredients. An individual's recipe takes time to form and what one does knows before-hand are the ingredients of the recipe. Unraveling the uniqueness hidden in children by educating them on the ingredients of their recipe is important in helping them realize their true potential. The goal should not be to target only the right ingredients; instead, it should be knowing the ingredients irrespective of whether right or wrong. Awareness of the behaviors exhibited helps parents develop a better understanding of their child. Although a concept that is difficult for children to grasp, it has its merits in raising awareness and self-belief. As regards my children, I noticed them being particularly receptive between the age group of 9 to14 years.

Patterns can also be noticed when the child is involved in other activities such as playing. We noticed such pattern with Rushil at 8 who often got irritated when called home from play. On the surface, it seemed obvious that not getting enough play-time was the culprit. Closer inspection revealed something different. He was a bundle of energy, often attracting attention from onlookers, with an innate ability to mingle with people across ages. His aura preceding, the neighborhood christened me 'Rushil's papa'! A creative and exploratory streak in him also made him restless. We were in for a surprise when we noticed that while he enjoyed being with other children, he did not really play with them. In an attempt to understand the root cause, we started engaging him in indoor games such as cards. He would get restless and attempt to do things differently and in the process end up breaking everybody else's rhythm. Though he preferred playing with us, it often ended in conflicts primarily because of his desire to do things differently. On the other hand, it was peaceful when the child was busy doing something creative like a project or organizing a cricket tournament among his peers.

Analyzing the patterns gathered helped us realize that people did not bother him but anything confined with rules was not his cup of tea. He needed freedom and flexibility to do things his way, and as parents who gave into his demands, we were his preferred playing partners. Further reflection into his toddler days made us realize that he enjoyed toys that enabled construction and destruction, Lego being his favorite. It not only exposed us to the concept of schemas (connecting type) but also gave us insight into his learning style (tactile). Tying it all helped us identify an ingredient of his recipe.

Dr. Shreeram Geet - The major factors that influence an individual recipe are family, financials, academics, skillset & psychology. A family is about supporting and encouraging. Financials are to do with stability and security. Academics concerns learning. Skillsets relate to interests and abilities. Psychology is about attitudes and personality.

Though not the one to doubt its efficacy, analyzing further reassured me of its significance. It could easily be applied to anybody with achievement in fields as diverse as sports, social, corporate etc. For a sports person, in addition to one's natural ability, knowing things such as learning style, motivating factors, goal setting, ability to control distraction etc. could be a differentiator. In short, it concerns things that work and things that don't. We can draw further similarities with legendary cricketer Sachin Tendulkar. There is no doubt that as a child, even Sachin Tendulkar may not have seen himself becoming the greatest batsman of his time. It must have been his parents and coach, who identified the ingredients ahead of time and guided him accordingly. While natural ability such as timing, reflex, techniques etc set him apart, there are those such as hard work, discipline, focus, commitment, that would have made him successful in any field he chose. Identifying the ingredients of one's recipe can often lead to the differentiation one looks for.

Dr. Shreeram Geet - Traditionally finding ones potential has a lot to do with exploring opportunities. Often getting into the right profession is a guessing game with mismatch in interest and assigned work. Some make mistakes only to succeed in figuring what suites them well. Finding one's true potential is a slow process, unless you have the stark imagination of being good at something.

Learning to identify the ingredients of my child's recipe required me to break from the norm and unlearn. It was not easy looking away from something that took years to practice. Be it their preference to an unstructured way of doing things or not following any rules, my children helped me challenge it all. Thinking about their distinctions often made me change my stance.

I realized that while a structured approach yielded less mistakes and improved chance of success, it minimizes the opportunity to improvise on the go and thus learn. It also makes one consistent and mechanical to some extent. Being unstructured keeps one on his or her toes. The same goes for rules; rules put up virtual walls that slows down creativity and confines one's thoughts. While my children are unable to explain why they choose to do certain things in certain ways or distinguish which is better, I have none-the-less decided that whatever helps them differentiate is probably the way to go.

While the long-term goal for my children is to independently identify the ingredients and nurture their own recipe, as of now, they need exposure and plenty of it. Simple self-awareness exercises during their summer break seem to keep them engaged. While one prefers exercises that are creative in nature, the other is often keen on knowing more about the self.

The Gist

Being observant has helped me learn a lot about my children. Tuning my parenting style to fit the needs of my children, I realized there being no such thing as perfect parent or a right or wrong style. There is thus no point in comparing with other parents though sharing notes and learning about their best practices has helped. While styles continue to evolve through ones learning and experiences, the important point is to be honest to one's style. Creating awareness of my parenting style has also helped my children understand my viewpoints.

Realizing that the soil provided as acceptance was heavy with evaluation, judgment, criticism, preaching and the likes was in itself a huge learning. A simple practice of looking at things as a whole made a big difference in how I accepted things. Given my children's uniqueness, comparisons were often baseless including comparison of experiences. Hopefully my children may have less difficulty accepting themselves.

Developing and nurturing the child now meant encouraging their uniqueness and making them self-aware. This implied looking for patterns in all aspects of development such as physical, mental, emotional or social. It is the one gift that I would like to give my children. Attempting understanding my recipe not only helped built awareness but also the commonality exhibited by children.

It is an opportunity to make a difference that I do not plan on missing.

An exercise on 'Learn Teach Learn'

Unraveling Oneself

a) Ever attempted retrospection? If so, which qualities best describe you, the individual? (Tips - Include your values, priorities, interests, strengths, weakness, personality etc.)

b) How much of what interests you overlap with your profession?

c) How would you describe your parenting style? (Tips - Accepting/ Rejecting, Responsive/Unresponsive, Ambitious/Conservative, Protective/Experimenting or Coaching/Helping)

d) Does your child occasionally remind you of your childhood? What similarities do you share with your child? (Tips - Intelligence, motor skills, voice coordination, behaviors etc.)

e) Have you ever asked your child to describe you as a parent?

Acceptance

f) How well do you accept yourself as an individual? (Tip - Use the retrospection done in earlier section)

g) Have you ever given a thought to the image of the child you have in your mind?

h) Do you have difficulty in accepting your child the way he/she is?

i) Do you tend to compare children, either with your childhood, siblings or their peers?

j) Give a thought to the three things that you expect from your child?

k) Has your child compared you with their friend's parents? How did it feel?

l) Do you help your child live his/ her dream?

Demystifying the Child

m)   What is the one gift that you would like to give your child?

n)   How well can you describe your child? (Tips - Exclude likes and preferences)

CHAPTER

3

Bridging the Gap

*'Actions speak louder than words.' ~ **Theodore Roosevelt***

Most of us from the corporate world have had the luxury of attending communication workshops where the focus often is on reducing tension, avoiding miscommunication and bringing harmony within the work place. All of these can be classified as outward communication. Right from childhood and well into adulthood, the focus in regards to communication is always on the outward part. We thus learn to be careful of what we say and think about it later causing our speech to be often unaligned with our thoughts. In other words, we choose to wrap our communication according to the profile of the person we are dealing with be it parents, subordinates, bosses or children with each requiring a different color. This situational communication creates misalignment and inconsistencies in one's thoughts and speech. We could term this style of communication as 'outside-in'.

As parents, we are gifted with reflectors in the form of children. They reflect everything parents' do and at times magnify it. This is when one realizes the need to be consistent in thought and speech. Being consistent often implies, aligning ones values, beliefs, thoughts, priorities etc. Irrespective of whom you talk to, you never feel the need to colour your conversation to suit the environment. It could be anyone right from your superior at work to the domestic help at home. Driven by your innermost of thoughts, you too in return get the other person's respect and gratitude.

All you need to do is be yourself which by itself implies being consistent and avoiding misalignment. This style of communication can be called 'inside-out'. Topics discussed in this chapter helps parents communicate 'inside-out' and reduce gaps that inhibit connect with children and vice versa.

Our Two Faces

'Your children will become who you are; so be who you want them to be.'
~David Bly

One of the things that often got me irritated was the children's situational behavior. They exhibited this peculiar brand of behavior when in places like a mall or an auditorium or when I was on the phone. Quite often, I believed their behavior was a result of their inability to contain their excitement. To make things worse, they expressed this affection only towards me. When such incidents became frequent, the initial reaction was to curtail visits- more of a spontaneous reaction than a solution. Left with no choice I resorted to explore. Little did I know, my exploration would boomerang and come back right at me!

On analyzing the situations that made me uncomfortable, I learnt that their behavior was more of a reaction that helped exercise their bargaining power. They were not just learning about my different faces but also learning the art of negotiation.

Inadvertently, I seemed to have nurtured this behavior upon asking them to be in their best behavior when we had guests over or were in a public place. People's reaction to our children's irrepressible behavior and its reflection on me as a parent played more on my mind than accepting them. My attempts at suppressing it inadvertently led to its developing different faces.

Once aware of my wrongdoing, it was not difficult noticing the presence of my multiple faces elsewhere. Whether, it was recognizing the liberty others had to make mistakes, or entitling maids to their share of vacation. I was nurturing double standards.

Corporate environment is an apt setting to observe such difference in behaviors. It is most noticeable when you compare people's behaviors when working up the hierarchy as opposed to working down. Then there are those who do not hesitate saying one thing in your presence and quite the opposite when you aren't around! These are by no means restricted to the office. You get to see them quite often at home. Case in point? Treatment meted out to daughters versus that to daughter-in-laws. Though generic in nature, such inconsistencies in behaviors lead to confusion and double standards. This is what forms the foundation of one's different faces.

Awareness of the multiple faces I projected and its impact on our children made me keen to bridge them and exhibit just one set of behaviors. I realized that simple acts such as honesty even in uncomfortable situations helped one accept things better. A genuine response no matter how stupid seems far more acceptable. Exhibiting multiple faces often implied I was holding back something that felt uncomfortable revealing. Interestingly, what is held back often becomes a topic of interest for others including children.

And while all this was on, I missed realizing that our children were doing more than just lending us an ear. Like sponges which absorb everything that gets tossed their way, they were absorbing and reciprocating the same through their behaviors. They tended to monitor behaviors and analyze actions. This constant analyzing of ones speech against ones actions is what creates parent's reputation and credibility with children. Being consistent not only helps children predict parent's behavior but also helps internalize the consequences of their actions. In other words, exhibiting consistency and transparency was the best means for the same to be reciprocated by children.

Dr. Bhooshan Shukla - Children are curious about their parents on subjects like what the latter do at work, did they ie parents have a normal childhood, is there hope for them, etc. They are constantly exploring and relating it to themselves. Hence it is important for parents to be honest regarding who they are.

I also noticed that children were not afraid of putting parents in a spot, especially when they noticed inconsistency in the latter's behavior. I recollect an instance when we were protesting against their school's exorbitant fee hike. At the time, a distant friend was looking to relocate and enquired about the schools in the locality. Before I was through covering the positives of their school, my daughter Rashi, then 12, took me aside and asked me 'Are you not concealing information, especially about your protest against the school'. I said, my protest does not mean that the school lack positives and that I planned on sharing the not–so-savory-details as well after I am done with the positives.

Dr. Yajyoti Singh - For a child, dual standard is not just about parents and their moods, but also about inconsistencies between them. These internal inconsistencies not only confuse the child but also make them manipulative. They know which parent to approach for what, and which mood present the best chances.

Delving further, I wondered why having multiple faces was common. One probable reason for the different behaviors could be rooted in the responsibilities exercised. At home, responsibility often encompasses everything. In the company of friends, the same is often shared and casual in nature. At work, responsibilities are clearly cut out with little ambiguity. For example, let us delve into the issue of ownership as one of the responsibility exercised across various situations. At home, the level of ownership is highest. At work, ownership is often limited to the area/task owned. In a public place the sense of ownership seem to dwindle with little realization that public property is in some ways our property. Differing sense of responsibility can confuse our sense of ownership and thus behavior. Could this be the main motive behind the inconsistent behaviors which when portrayed regularly starts developing into ones different faces?

Overcoming one's multiple faces thus imply having a core set of responsibilities that can influence behaviors irrespective of the situations. This core set of responsibilities would not just be an amalgamation of ones believes and values but also how well one accepts oneself. Thus not knowing the behavior expected from oneself, could be attributed to the lack of understanding of ones values and beliefs. Being honest to ones' core implies consistency in behavior irrespective of the situation.

While creating a benchmark is important from an individual standpoint, sharing it with the family is important for consistency. If being a responsible citizen is important to you, bring it to your child's notice. This not only helps the child understand the behavior you exhibit but also helps in identifying deviations.

Dr. Shreeram Geet - Values and beliefs are not the easiest to retain. Though individual in nature, surviving situational strain often requires support from family. The family plays an important role in living ones values and hence sharing it is of prime importance.

As always, I had to be reminded of not going overboard and aiming for the "Mr. Clean" kind of image. Instead, the key was to be honest and consistent. Though I had little control on what my children imbibed, portraying a larger than life image could be challenging for children to deal with. In some ways, it is like setting high standards, which might quite likely distance the child. It may also seed the feeling of not being up to parents' expectations. I believe it is important for children to know that parents are not perfect and are as human as they are. Be it lack of discipline, being unorganized, irresponsible or not focused, I have had my fair share. I was never a perfect child and have little chances of being a perfect parent. This is a fact that my children need to know.

Having multiple faces is common and not something to lose sleep on. However, children would any day prefer having parents who are consistent and predictable. This not only helps connect with people around you but also to your inner self. There is no reason one shouldn't be proud of oneself.

Juggling roles

'Do three things well, not ten things badly.'~ ***David Segrove***

My activities after reaching home from work, involved walking through our children's task list for the day. Being quite extensive, slippages were high which I would highlight to Anita along with its importance. This invariably resulted in unpleasant and uncomfortable exchanges. Despite our best efforts, things did not progress along intended lines.

Relief then came from a very unusual source: the understanding of the varied roles one plays and the associated priorities. What surprised us was the range of mini roles we parents play. Mini roles can be described as the different roles played within the parenting umbrella. It varied from being their caretaker to cook, teacher to assistant, friend to coach, lawmaker, promoter, critic and so on. On an average, Anita played at least 6 mini roles on any given day. Switching between these was complicated and confusing, calling for effective juggling.

Developing an understanding also helped us dig into our personal past. I remember my Mom giving me a hard time with regards to studies. She watched over us siblings while being engrossed reading the newspaper in the middle of her snooze. When dad got back from work, she would unfailingly relay our day's achievement effectively summarize in one sentence "The child has done nothing". This often cost us our playtime- very precious to us then! It was what kept us engaged in school, losing which was frustrating to say the least.

As children, we had little understanding of what Mom was trying to achieve. We instead thought of her as the instigator. On days when dad came home with a short fuse, she would also be our savior. This behavior confounded things further as we failed to understand why she would complain in the first place.

Dr. Yajyoti Singh - A common issue with most households is of one parent doing too much. Homemakers in their guilt of not doing enough end up juggling the most. Living up to the expectations dumped on them, they end up compromising on the quality of parenting. Those who rely majorly on outsourcing may not feel stressed though they are likely to miss out on the intense interaction between parent and child.

Prioritizing the roles to be played can help in being more effective. Knowing individual traits can also help in identifying the role one plays. A dominant parent may need to become liberal and a compassionate parent cannot remain so throughout the day.

Having no clue of what parents were trying to achieve, it was easy surmising such behaviors as negative. I also knew of friends who struggled to rationalize their parent's behaviors, ending up carrying remorse. While some of this role-play may be filled with remorse for the child, there is no running away from it. The invariable question that popped-up was "how can I make it easy for children to understand our intentions?"

Though Anita understood the concept, she was not too convinced of the benefits that knowing the roles one plays, offered. It was quite clear that Anita was stretching to cover as many mini roles as possible. As if driven by instinct, along with the daily routines, she was also attending problems as they erupted. It was important for her to get the children ready for school, cook for them, help them with their studies, do the household chores, take them out etc. Areas with no problems grabbed little of her attention while focused ones took away majority of her time. While this was certainly one way of dealing with things, another would be to become aware of the different mini roles one plays. Awareness of the mini roles being played helps justify the role being played and thus times spend. In short, why should problems dictate how one spends quality time with one's child? Priorities should instead. Where one is worried about playing too many roles, it is then time to list, prioritize and share. These can help drop lower priority roles in favour of higher ones.

To elaborate on the above, take for instance the case of a parent playing a teacher's role with two children. While the younger one is independent in regards to studies, the elder one requires supervision. Leveraging the understanding that children are unique in their own way, parents can choose to give personalized attention as per their need (ensuring the parenting style stays consistent). Keeping this in mind, one may want to drop playing the role of a teacher for the independent child while keeping it for the other. A conscious decision of sharing roles between parents or outsourcing the less important ones too can help the parent focus on the right roles. Given my experimental nature, not all roles were meant for me. It was important to pick the roles that brought pleasure and enjoyment for all, children, Anita and me as well provide some relief to Anita. Stretching to accommodate as many roles as possible was not helping either of us, resulting in going overboard and losing effectiveness.

Role-play, though simple had additional benefits. It could further be divided into two areas, scope and limits. The scope for a given role outlines the responsibility of the role. In other words, it helps identify the specific activities that are targeted as part of the role. Along with providing focus, it helps avoid stretching and overdoing. Limits on the other hand help in compartmentalizing of the roles by providing guardrails, thus restraining parents from spilling over into other roles.

Scope of a role - While outlining the scope for the teacher mini-role, I listed all the activities that seemed relevant such as preparing mind map for the chapters, watching educational videos, weekly tests, maintaining list of new words, practicing mathematics etc. While the list was structured and focused on all-around development, it was exhaustive. It spoke more about proving my abilities as a teacher and less about what the child really needed. I missed the point of developing child's interest in studies. Pairing the list down to two or three activities meant keeping only those that brought about the biggest impact while dropping the rest. It helped avoid stretching our resources. A practical scope was thus formed, anything beyond fell outside the purview of the role.

Limits of a role - As for the limits, let us take the example of a child getting adverse remark in the school diary for not completing homework. The usual response of parents seeing such remarks is to get worked-up and punish the child by curtailing playtime. While this reaction seems normal on the surface, digging deeper and compartmentalizing helped viewing it differently. By deciding to curtail playtime, role boundaries of a teacher were getting crossed. Deciding on playtime is in some ways out of bounds for a teacher role, thus parents are forced to look for consequences that fall under the teacher's role. Limits help compartmentalize and define boundaries, thus forcing solutions within set boundaries.

It took Anita some time to confess that she often crossed boundaries by crisscrossing roles. She measured every aspect of the child using only one yardstick, education. This often was a good enough excuse to curtail the child's TV time, playtime or Xbox time. In some ways, she over-exercised her teacher's role to make the child feel guilty. Having learnt about compartmentalizing, she plans to put it to use.

Dr. Bhooshan Shukla - It is important for parents to see them as roles and not confuse roles with their inner existence. If a child misbehaves, then becoming a disciplinarian is the need of the hour. Worrying about losing the child and not doing what is necessary is hardly an option. Being aware and willing to play roles is very important.

As part of implementation, it was important educating children on what we were trying to achieve. Lack of insight on the different roles parent's play could give children the impression of parents stamping their authority. Such impressions can easily cause drifts between parent and children. Children irrespective of their age should be taken into confidence. They may not always comprehend it, but with time, the pieces will fall in place. Explaining the different role will help in understanding parents viewpoint and thus the goal. Also it helps set expectation on how parent plan to be involved in a particular role.

Dr. Shreeram Geet - Parents think right, they are autonomous dictatorial teacher. Very few believe in nurturing the child, though not a new concept it is a spreading concept. The key is passive parenting with active involvement. Passive parenting means letting the child continue what he/she likes to do and active involvement is about spending time and engaging the child.

One of the biggest changes that understanding roles brought about was how I expressed my love and affection for children. Anita never let her love for children be affected by the role she played. She made it a point to provide love and care as part of her prime responsibility. She believed, children need their share of love and affection and it was important that parents be explicit about it. A child's day should start and end, seeing parent in that role. At the end of the day, they need to know that parents care for them, and will always be there for them. Irrespective of the kind of discussion she had with children, they were assured that none of it would affect their relationship.

Thanks to these roles, I learnt to detach myself irrespective of how mad I felt and wish the children a good night, further strengthening the bond between us.

Tangling conversations
'Silence is also conversation.' ~**Ramana Maharshi**

As the children grew up, healthy conversations became rare. It was common for conversation to deviate from the issue ending up in dismay and leading nowhere. Eventually those verbal conflicts lead to egoistic clashes with both parties keen on stressing and proving their point. Such conversations, instead of helping bringing the children closer were creating a rift with those involved gathering an impression of others being non-cooperating. An invisible barrier was starting to develop.

Clueless on how to overcome it, we sought external help. Listening to the arguments of those involved and going through recorded conversation led to forming a few conclusions. Conversations were being approached with vested interests with the intent of justifying individual viewpoint while conflict resolution was put on the back burners. Discussions often got into legalities, tossing around and grabbing every other irrelevant point that came their way. It was also observed that, whatever listening took place was focused on identifying gaps in the others person's argument. It soon started to become obvious as to why the simplest of issues got pushed away to be resolved on another day.

As learnt, one of the common reasons for conversations going haywire was tangling conversations. Such conversations lacked focus and often drifted. Participants in such conversations were more focused on standing their ground and proving their point. In doing so they argue and counter-argue on every possible point widening the conversation to the point where it bloats, loses focus and gets unhealthy. An unhealthy conversation easily translates into ego conflicts yielding little.

Dr. Bhooshan Shukla - Russell Peters in his comedy show talks about Indian parents being perfect salesperson. They are selling everything, even when talking to their children they are at their salesperson best. While there is nothing wrong in being a salesperson, the least you need to do is to hear the other person. Conversations are meant to be two-way. How much have you heard before you opened your mouth?

One way to avoid conversations getting tangled is doing them "in spirit". In a spirited conversation, people are willing to understand the other person's arguments in addition to proving their point. Such conversations are not about winning or losing but about making sense. With no room for ego, such conversations tend to focus on the problem at hand. In addition, they also provide learning opportunities to those involved. Such discussions, that focuses on understanding other's viewpoints lead to quicker resolution. Learning to have effective and thus fruitful conversations helped Anita, the children and me.

It is also important to realize when conversations are not headed anywhere. On such occasions, it is wiser to just pullout of such conversations. Rude though it may sound, it does less damage to the relationship.

Dr. Shreeram Geet - Children are receptive to what parents convey, especially when it is followed with details and examples. If the same is passed as comment, children tend to ignore thinking of parents' words as those resembling a broken record. A well thought original and simplified dialogue would always have audiences.

Here is an example of a conversation between a parent and a child that focuses on legality and lacks spirit.

--------- **Start Conversation** ------------

Parent : Millie, did you notice your overall grades were lower as compared to the last semester

Millie : What…? They are not that bad. Everybody in class fared badly.

Parent : This is not about students in your class, it is about you. You seem to have a lot of distractions these days.

Parent : You seem to be spending most of your time on the Internet. I wonder how that helps your grades. I plan on activating parental control and rationing your usage.

Millie : You always do this to me, I have no freedom. My friends have no such restrictions.

Parent : Maybe your friends continue to get good grades, which is why they may not have such restrictions.

Parent : Do not talk of freedom; this is not about freedom. It is all a result of your lack of motivation; you still haven't figured out what you want to do with your career.

Millie : I hate you.

--------- **End Conversation** ------------

Such conversations were common in our family. In hindsight, it is easy to notice the conversation oscillating between lower grades, Internet usage, personal freedom, comparison of restrictions and lack of motivation. In the end, one wonders where it all started and what did one achieve from such a conversation. What this conversation lacks is spirit from both sides and thus a focus. By not being accepting of each other's arguments, the conversation struggles to stay focused, gets dragged all over and in the process tangles and becomes unsolvable.

A probable approach to dealing with such situations is for both parties to agree and have conversations that stay focused on the topic. In this particular example, since the focus of conversation is lower grades, the participants should try and avoid deviating from it. All other viewpoints about Internet usage, being too restrictive, lack of motivation are valid in their own right but have no value to offer as part of this discussion other than complicate things further. The right thing here is to bring up these topics separately and deal with them accordingly.

Here is a revised conversation focusing on topic of overall grades.

--------- **Start Revised Conversation** ------------

Parent : Millie, did you notice your overall grades were lower compared to the last semester?

Millie : Yes, I did notice it. Everybody in class fared badly.

Parent : This is not about students in your class, it is about you. Do you know the reasons for the lower grades?

Millie : I have no idea, I put in the same amount of effort. Teachers also mentioned, this year will be tough.

Parent : Did you get your answer sheets reviewed? Is there anything obvious?

Millie : I did get the sheets though I could not find anything obvious.

Parent : Let us together examine it and see if there are any patterns.

Parent : During the next open day, we should also talk to your teachers and find if they have any observations to share.

Millie : Ok.

--------- **End Revised Conversation** -----------

Since this conversation focuses on the topic on hand, it does not stray and thus achieves its goal.

If one could relate to having similar conversations, there is nothing alarming. This is probably a common territorial behavior and one of the easiest to address. When approaching discussions, we must constantly remind ourselves that irrespective of what gets discussed, the goal is to have a healthy conversation. Children shall continue with their natural tendency of pushing limits. Not all our conversations reach amicable resolution. Over time we learn to accept that to 'agree to disagree' too is an important aspect of communication.

Widening rift

'Sometimes it falls upon a generation to be great, you can be that generation.' ~ *Nelson Mandela*

It was that time in our child's life where the need for some heart-to-heart talk was imperative. Irrespective of how close you are to your children, such situations are none-the-less uncomfortable for most parents.

While browsing the newspaper, I chanced upon an article 'Teen Pregnancies up by 50%' ([4]Tarini Peshawaria). It reminded me of the long overdue private talk with our elder child. The real shockers was that majority of the youngsters

---

[4]Tarini Peshawaria, " Docs worried about rising teen pregnancy, self-abortion in Gurgaon", http://timesofindia.indiatimes.com/life-style/people/Docs-worried-about-rising-teen-pregnancy-self-abortion-in-Gurgaon/articleshow/21274442.cms

belonged to educated families like ours. Another alarming fact was that it was the boyfriends/friends and not parents who accompanied the girls to the hospital! Why this disconnect when these youngsters are from families similar to ours? It was rather obvious that most parents like us were procrastinating having conversation with children about growing up.

Dr. Bhooshan Shukla - It is not that parents are unaware of the generation gap, instead they are scared of it. Children, convinced that parents will never understand prefer hiding than confiding things.

Keen on exploring the 'Generation gap' further, I wondered why we find it difficult to relate to any generation other than ours. Is it that we feel the need to experience it to relate? Alternatively, is it because we struggle to invest time and understand its significance?

For convenience, I often blamed the younger generation for the things they did differently. Though deep inside, there were hardly any doubts of this being no fault of theirs. This rift is probably a result of our specie's constant endeavor to improve upon ourselves. Whether it is about technological advances, and the information age, enhanced quality of life or ascent towards individuality, the youth is at the forefront to embrace the new trends and propel them further. If this generation gap were like a chasm then its depth could be the parents' doing. Though children may have some clue, majority of it will be nothing but history. The question that manifested itself is, will I be ready to immerse my pride, subdue my ego and take the plunge to bridge this chasm?

Contrary to popular belief, not everybody struggles with this rift. I know people who are open-minded and see opportunity in the change that lie ahead. These are early adaptors, who grab the opportunity and embrace change. Such people fuel new trends and create the kind of music, books, TV shows, fashion trends, gadgets, fast food etc. that the youth learns to associate with.

Despite our differences, Anita being conservative and I being liberal, both feel fortunate having experienced shifts in our lifestyle, communities and work place. One feels at a loss on seeing the current youth and the very little exposure their parents may have. How could one bridge such chasm(s) where the shifts are not just technological, but in a whole bunch of other areas such as mobility of lives, increased economic opportunities, surge in middle-class income and consequent spending, experimenting with relationship, arranged marriages and its sanctity and so on. I remember Rushil's friend who in his 9th grade had been through 2 relationships. For some reason, his parents seemed oblivious. While we saw value in individuals experiencing relationships, we were uncomfortable with the idea of children so young experiencing it. The thought often left me wondering on what one could do to avoid such disconnects.

Dr. Bhooshan Shukla - The age that parents believe their children are ready to learn about things has reduced by about 5 years. The generation gap, which was once 20-25 years, has now reduced to 7. Siblings born with an age gap of 7 years are likely to be in different generations.

From what I could gather, how one chooses to deal with such situations depend upon one's ability to learn and adapt. One's learning and experiences, which have guided them for years may become their limitation. Conditioned as it is to a particular thought process, one is forced to think and act in a certain manner. Learning and unlearning thus become difficult and restrains the adoption of newer ways of life. Our inability to be like them contributes to our lack of understanding of their generation thus widening the rift. In other words, parents need to learn to see life through the eyes of their children.

Dr. Bhooshan Shukla - Humans are the only species that have a generation gap. Those who develop an understanding by accepting it are likely to leverage their child as a window to the next generation and learn.

For the longest time I wanted to be my children's friend. Unsure, if it was really about friendship or investing for the long run especially their teen years. However, every decision we made against their wish jeopardized that position. Our relationship was not of equals as they did not call the shots or set the rules, or for that matter set limits or decide on the consequences. While I wished for them to confide in me, reciprocating the same was off limits. How then was I thinking of being their friend?

Adapting and adjusting to outlook that are different from what one grows with may not come easily to everyone. Generation gaps are for real and awareness of the things that drive today's children is a must. Though I do not enjoy watching their kind of teenage/detective shows or like shooting adversaries on XBox, I make it a point to hang out with them doing things like watching their T.V. shows, knowing their opinion, being part of their network, learning about things that bother them, attempting to listen to their kind of music etc. My children expect logic and reasoning in everything they do. They are not afraid of asking tough question and are unlikely to follow blindly. Having children follow practices by inducing fear is not something that will work with them. Trying to make them live the way their parents did would mean slowing them down and disconnecting them from their generation. It would also imply taking away their ability to make mistakes. Like previous generations, they need freedom and where accompanied with education may help avoid probable pitfalls. They are bound to make mistakes and should be encouraged as long as they learn.

Dr. Yajyoti Singh - When it comes to generation gap, the thing that affects parents most is their value system getting compromised. Like with most generations, the youth are just going with the flow of what is happening around them. Convincing children on why they should imbibe their parents' value system would require them to be role models.

This chasm is not getting shallower; instead, it is firmly growing roots within our family set-up finding grudging acceptance. We are now starting to see dating and live-in relationship gaining acceptance among the youth. With things not getting easier any time soon, one has to face the onslaught even as grandparents. Choosing to stay in the shell, cocooned from the world, resisting this change might hardly be an option. I feel it is better to adapt early and face less resistance. Hopefully our children will learn a thing or two and most likely do a better job when their time comes.

Dr. Yajyoti Singh - Children are anyways going to do what they feel right, given half a chance they will be more than willing to confide in their parents. Unfortunately, parents freak out and close the doors of communication.

The Gist

I always fancied this notion of having a connect with my children though neither preferred confiding in me. I suspected communication gaps to be the culprit. In reality, gaps lay between my beliefs and actions that did not go unnoticed by my children. It not only caused confusion and inconsistency but also made me less predictable.

Developing an understanding of the various mini roles was a necessity. It helped reduce stress and focus on the right roles. Sharing facts with children and raising their awareness helped reduce displeasure. The best learning was showing them we cared, expressing love and affection irrespective of the situation.

It required little efforts to take the simplest of conversations and get them entangled. Resolving them meant viewing them as learning opportunities and ensuring it was done in the right spirit. Even now, conversations do get tangled, but knowing when to back off has helped. Conversations resulting in fruitful discussions are certainly on the rise.

For a while, the generation gap seemed like a child's wrong doing, until reality sunk in. Now, I am of the opinion that if the gap were like a chasm then its depth could be the parent's making. Unlike most occasions, our learning and experiences impede in bridging the gap. I do not believe in adapting to all that the children are going through, but certainly want to be aware of the things that are driving them.

Topics addressed in this chapter are focused on parents and are thus easy to implement. If communication is about tuning to other person's wavelength then parents need to tune their wavelength.

An exercise on 'Bridging the Gap'

Our Two Faces

a)   Is consistency a virtue that you like in others? In what areas would you consider yourself consistent?

b)   Would it matter if your children hid things from you? Have you tried unearthing your reputation amongst your children?

c)   Do you expect children to be on their best behavior when you have guests at home or in a public place?

d)   Would like a little surprise? Ask your children about your various moods.

Juggling roles

e)   Are you spread thin? Which of the roles you play as a parent are most important?

f)   Is your love for your children unconditional? How often do you hug or kiss them?

g)   Are you effective as a parent? If not what could be done better?

Tangling conversation

h)   Do you consider children equal when having a conversation?

i)   Does your conversations with children yield results or get pushed for another day?

j)   Do you speak like a salesperson, always tying to prove your point with children?

Widening rift

k) Have you ever had private/personal conversations with children? Try to recollect.

l) How much time do you spend sharing their interests, connecting with their generation?

m) Do you consider your children to be your friends?

n) Do you confide in your children?

Being the Coach

'A coach is someone who can give correction without causing resentment.'
~ John Wooden

In retrospect, if time ever presented me with the luxury of changing one thing in the past, I would opt to have a coach. Fortunate enough to have made mistakes, I learnt though from only a few. I wish, I had learnt more...

Dr. Shreeram Geet - Where the shoe pinches and how to solve it, a coach knows. A coach need not be a winner but needs to know the game. They are required to be supportive, empathetic, and strategic in approach. The ability to find faults and improvise is a must. Instructions along with directions need to be single-handed; having multiple coaches is never recommended.

Everybody needs a coach, a guru, until they learn to coach themselves. This person has to have the time and ability to analyze, see the big picture and be the guiding star. Parents are naturally most suited for the role till the child finds a coach of his/ her liking.

Coaching as I see it is about stepping back and approaching without preset expectations. It is about being a mirror, nurturing the learner's uniqueness and thus helping them understand themselves. Giving them exposure to assimilate their own experiences and expand their horizon. Guiding them and yet having them make their own decisions. Giving the freedom to make mistakes, while focusing on the takeaways.

Dr. Bhooshan Shukla - It is important not to mix up mentoring with coaching. Mentoring is where you walk the path and shine a light for others. As a coach you walk with them, gain experience training people and know where the pitfalls lie. What children need is a parent who can coach objectively, be accepting and know when to detach.

Occasionally, I tend to recalibrate my actions based on my children's feedback. Once I asked them how they would describe me as a father. A couple of minutes later they summed all in just one word, guiding. Holding back my emotions, I could barely thank them in a cracked voice!

Growth Beyond the Comfort Zone

'We find comfort among those who agree with us – growth among those who don't.' ~ **Frank A. Clark**

If life were a race, some of my attempts to give the children a head start might have actually proved counterproductive resulting in them standing a few meters further from the starting line. Taking cues from my struggles, I made it my priority to ensure that my wards did not go through similar experiences. In doing so, the child's experiences were cut short due to my conditioning them in ignorance.

While I took pride in shielding them, what they really needed was my support. Mistaking shielding for supporting, I realized that doing so barred them from experiencing failure, learning from challenges and maintaining a positive mindset. Exposure on the other hand not only prepared them for the journey called life but also helped them understand themselves.

It is hard to contemplate on what I would be without my experiences. I am certain of its playing an integral part in defining my identity. How could I take that away from my children?

Pitfalls of the "Comfort Zone"

'Life begins at the end of your comfort zone.' - **Neale Donald Walsch**

With a practical approach to life, I never believed in pampering children. Upon understanding the various dimensions of comfort zone, I was exposed to my ignorance. While I did score on some counts such as giving them exposure, introducing them to change, avoiding being over sympathetic, there were also those areas where I had gone negative perceiving them to be nothing more than an extension, over indulging and uncalled for intervention.

I doubt whether my children understood the concept of a comfort zone or its implications. They seemed to be attracted to the warmth it provided which was something I seeded through my behavior. In my pursuit to give them the best, I often went overboard in comforting them and creating smaller comfort zones called sympathy zones. By taking the child's likings and preferences far too seriously, I inadvertently cut short their experiences. I realized that their preferences were not a result of having tried out the available options before settling on what they liked. Instead, it was driven by their desire to not try and be bailed out. Such sympathy zones shielded the child and deprived them of much-needed experience which overtime grows into behaviors that translates into comfort zones.

I remember driving home the point with a simple experiment. Like most children, my kids too have a liking for ice cream though blindly biased towards Mango or Chocolate. Trying to explain what they were missing, especially with such a vast range of flavors though fell on deaf ears. Children's behavior can at times be puzzling. Take them to a toy store and they appear confused. They struggle to pick just one toy and while in an ice cream parlor they know precisely what they want! To make things worse whenever their grandparents visited us, they brought along flavors that the children liked.

The point I was trying to make seemed to be lost. I decided to have ice-cream evenings over the weekends with a catch that only the flavor of the day would be offered. Both initially resisted the idea and let it pass a few times. Then Rushil broke loose, giving up and enjoying the experience. For Rashi, resistance any further was futile and she too gave in. These exercises were simple and easy to execute. Deciding on something without experiencing the available options was like pigeonholing. It not only undercut their experiences but also limited their view. When repeated under different scenarios, the learning started to become more plausible.

I am sure our children would have felt let down for some time. Unfortunately, it did not end there. Taken to any restaurant, all they would want is pasta, pancakes, waffle or burger. Further, they did an excellent job at making us feel guilty, leaving the only escape route to give in. Anxious to overcome the situation, we set a thumb rule of completing all negotiations prior to reaching the restaurant. Once at the venue, children always had an upper hand. Considering everybody's desires, we took turns within the family in deciding the venue and the menu; the other members of the family had to willingly co-operate or risk losing their turn. Another option was to approach restaurants based on their cuisine and set one's sights only on those dishes that were relevant to the cuisine. Options that induce change and are amicable in nature often seem favorable to children. Then there were those occasional outbursts where being persuasive helped in getting over them.

In some ways, these feel like games that children play. The ploy set, the actors singled out, lines well rehearsed and outcome visualized each step is carried out precisely. Busting these implies recognizing the pattern and understanding the rational behind them. Irrespective of the approaches deployed (positive reinforcement, withdrawing privileges, consequences, ignoring, etc.) having a fun element makes it easier to change ones behavior.

Another thing that we did well in addition to overcoming sympathy zones was giving children exposure. Children at times have little realization of what their behaviors has in store for others. When planning a vacation, the first thing they would ask is 'how many stars does the hotel have'. This gave us a tough time when we decided to visit remote places with limited facilities. But just a few days of stay up close with nature and numerous first time experiences such as walking in the footsteps of the apex predator, getting mesmerized by the sight of zillions of stars shining down from the night sky, suspecting any shiny object in the dark, slumbering to the howling calls etc., opened them up for future visits. We learnt that the best way to persuade children was to approach such visits with a priority. Outlining the priority helped them understand what to expect. Realizing that not all visits are about luxury and comfort, they are now more than willing to trade for newer experiences. In fact, these visits have been a hit, with their friends wanting to accompany them.

Dr. Shreeram Geet - Nuclear families and high rises have confined children to apartments. Often the only people they meet other than in school, are parents and siblings. With limited exposure, they are bound to be in their comfort zone. Protected and shielded, they have little exposure to normal life. Preoccupied with gadgets and identifying new car models, we think of them being smarter. Simple things such as taking the kid to the market or involving them in household activities like cooking can give them the required exposure.

It was not easy accepting my overindulgence. In hindsight, I surely did a lot of it assuming I was passing down some of my traits such as not watching Television and thus limiting their exposure to a collection of 100+ animation DVD's. With satellite television too, there was insistence on watching educational channels such as Discovery and National Geographic. Not being much of a gadget person, I assumed them being neither, only to be proven wrong, yet again. There were other situations as well where I had stretched my quirks and applied it on them such as my obsession with hygiene which included a blanket ban on petting stray animals or playing in the mud. It started to seem less about them and more about my pet peeves.

Dr. Yajyoti Singh - A large chunk of parents go overboard in comforting children. Whether it is about buying toys or handing gadgets, there is an abundance of overindulgence. It is not just limited to materialistic indulgence or cognitive stimulation but also where penalizing or disciplining is concerned.

While we were not afraid of rocking the boat, we surely had our share of going with the flow. We often got caught up in overcoming daily tasks while overlooking the need for improvisation. A common routine most visible in every household with children is the amount of effort put every morning, in preparing the kids for school. We tend to behave like alarm clocks providing continuous reminders of all the activities to be performed by the child. Interestingly, it not only epitomizes teamwork but guarantees participation from all. Every person adds value without pausing for a moment and asking the obvious: does this help the child in the long run, especially those in secondary school?

I was not sure, what ignited this risk-averse behavior. Was it our tendency to worry about consequences without attempting to understand them or our lack of foresight? The most likely consequence here could be that the child struggles for a few days and at worst may miss few a days of school in a year. It took lots of persuasion to introduce and highlight the benefits of periodically increasing a child's exposure and its outweighing possible consequences. By preempting and exposing them to change, we give them an opportunity to learn in a controlled environment. On the other hand, it also presented an opportunity for us to know about our child's behavior in given situations.

Dr. Bhooshan Shukla - There are two big pitfalls a) too much intervention and b) excessive stimulation. Parents have difficulty-seeing children as an independent entity with its own needs. They often see them as an extension of themselves. Essentially catering to their inner child and pampering themselves, they miss looking at the real child.

While Anita was worried about the children's reaction when going through frequent change, she had a point. To avoid overdoing we agreed that the opportunity to learn should outweigh the risk of causing discomfort to children. While change often brought opportunity, it took time for learnings to be imbibed. There was no point over reacting and introducing more than a couple of changes at a time. It would likely do more harm than good. Moreover, ample time had to be given to accept and get accustomed to new ideas.

Dr. Bhooshan Shukla: For children to deal with change, they need a sense of constancy inside. The right age varying with individuals, is difficult to pinpoint. Having a stable environment until puberty is very important as it is then that they start to form their identity.

Just as over-comforting may not be the norm for all parents, the same applies to children's comfort zone(s). There are those who willingly embrace change, explore and stretch themselves. Such children need to be made aware of their strengths and it being an ingredient of their recipe. As for children who resist change and prefer to be in their comfort zone, they need to be educated on how it limits their ability. I believe, children should be presented with the opportunity to stumble early on so they learn to run when it matters the most. Since this is not something that can be addressed in one go, it makes sense to go slow, take baby steps and get them over the so-called sympathy zones one step at a time.

Maintaining a Positive Outlook

'You cannot have a positive life and a negative mind.' ~ *Joyce Meyer*

Interestingly both Anita and I preferred our childhood over what we see of the current generation. It seems being a child is not fun anymore. Despite so much going in their favor, they seem to have so little time for themselves. Shadowed by stress and tempered by strained relationships, childhood has evolved significantly. The simplicity of life has been traded for materialistic luxury. Childhood is just not the same, with competition becoming boundless and independence clipped by the insecurities of urban living. This puts extra pressure on making home the place where children seek solace.

Stress, though an unwelcome guest seem to flourish in every dwelling. Interestingly, it has evolved to take different forms based on ones convenience such as self-pity, denial, non-acceptance, dissatisfaction etc. Likewise, there are different ways in which people deal with it, some choosing to ignore it, others taking its positive side while some sulk it out. Anita and I had our own myriad different ways of dealing with stress and it all boiled down to our moods. There was thus a need for consistency in the way we managed stress, especially with regard to our actions.

Dr. Yajyoti Singh - While children may seem stressed, parents are the ones more stressed. The measure of parenting is often the child's performance, which gets relayed to the child. Individual stress is also on the rise, be it financial, personal, or professional. The most sought-after solution to allay such fears is securing your child's education. While for a child the prime stress of all might be academic, children are quite likely to not take pressure, if parents were to not absorb and relay them.

Given our family chemistry, majority of our grievances sourced from two areas 'Using education as a yardstick' and 'Internalizing of discipline'. Applying the understanding from 'Juggling roles' (discussed in prior chapter) helped alleviate the use of education as a yardstick. Coaching children to 'Own their actions' (discussed in subsequent chapter) helped in targeting the issue of internalizing discipline.

In addition to knowing what caused the most grievances, there was a need to create a positive environment at home. The areas that helped were a) Being appreciative, b) Embracing criticism and, c) Nurturing one's energy sources.

- **Being appreciative** - It was important for us to find appreciation, even in the most distressing of situations. This did not mean tolerating or ignoring children's mistakes; instead it implied coaching ourselves to look at the positives. I recollect an incident where our children at 15 and 13 were to babysit 2 pet dogs for an afternoon. The scene on our return was straight out of a horror movie! It was like the aftermath of a hurricane or a tsunami with our house turned almost upside-down! The armrests of the couch were ripped out, the rug slit open, the retractable leash shreded to pieces. What we saw left us stunned and speechless! It took a while to react. Thankfully, the children and our pets were fine.

Focusing on the positives, we advised them on how they could do better in future- a clear departure from the usual where unable to control our emotions we would go ballistic. That night was different as we directed our anger towards salvaging whatever we could. Staying up late, we stitched and pasted back the pieces of foam and put the whole thing together. Despite our best efforts, the sofa had a renewed Frankenstein monster-like look. Lack of the proverbial "blame game" did make us proud of our behavior; we could for once, also discern a veil of regret around our children.

We realized that when made to sound more like an experience rather than an offence, children accepted it willingly. This was a pleasant departure from the normal defensive response to a blame apportioning exercise.

- **Embracing criticism** - Having travelled quite a bit, one of the things that stood out amongst us Indians when compared to other nationals is our inability to stomach criticism. This tendency is prevalent not just in the corporate sector but also within families, communities etc. Our family too was not an exception. The positive aspect was that everybody had the freedom to criticize be it children criticizing parents or parents criticizing children.

As for things that needed to be set right, there were quite a few. Conversations were hardly constructive and often resulted in upset family members. Comments taken personally often worked up defenses. Even sensitive conversations were not rewarded a private audience.

For individuals to deal competitively in a world without borders, embracing criticism becomes vital. Criticism when viewed positively is like a favor of sorts. It is like presenting others with an opportunity to better their selves and as such, should be encouraged and thanked. There is no better place than home for such learning to start.

Bhooshan Shukla - Criticizing is a very emotional process and experience. Children criticize parents when angry and it is the latter's reaction to such criticism that is the child's essential learning. Talking about it or recognizing it does not help learn. What does though is learning by practicing.

- **Nurturing one's energy sources** - Most of my acquaintances nurtured hobbies. I for one never had any. Having nothing to lean on, I loved contemplating and there was always that little more to unravel. Staying positive made me realize the need to know my energy sources. Those who nurture their energy sources find it easy to recuperate or stay positive when depressed or dejected. Generically speaking, extroverts draw energy from people, while introverts draw energy from within. Probable energy source could mean being with nature, digging into books, working out, meditation, religious devotion etc. Making a conscious attempt to understand my energy source helped nurture and refine them. Those struggling to identify their energy sources may want to cultivate hobbies, which are considered good energy sources.

Bhooshan Shukla - Most children know their energy sources quite instinctively and is the reason why they pursue them. It is unlikely that such activities remain the same as one grows older. It is important for them to find their energy sources, and not something that needs to be told.

For our daughter Rashi, then 15, having a sense of accomplishment toward the close of day meant a lot. Unable to achieve it often left her irritated. To make things worse, she would immerse herself either in Television or the Internet and end up feeling miserable. Once out of rhythm and dejected, she would try to suppress it instead of overcoming it. This downward spiral eventually ended in a quarrel. Having noticed the pattern, I highlighted how being unable to accomplishing things caused annoyance. Having realized this, she now draws herself to books whenever she wants to overcome an unpleasant situation. Explaining the same hypothesis to Rushil then 13 helped him apply it differently. He learnt that physically demanding games energized and excited him as opposed to watching TV or browsing the net, relatively energy draining activities. Recognizing this, he realigned his daily activities such that studies always followed physical activities.

A recap of the aspects that help reduce stress and aid in maintaining a positive environment at home

- The ability to find appreciation even in the most distressed of situations

- Encouragement to constructive criticism and viewing critics as well-wishers

- Making a conscious attempt to understand one's energy sources and leveraging them in times of distress.

On making the above changes, results became apparent. There was a hitch though. We got into the habit of pinpointing each other's not-so-positive behavior every now and then. It did help but what was really needed was a simple way to measure our conduct.

A simple tool that we put together helped view our action. The idea was to sum the daily activities into three sets of moments. The first would be the 'Cheerful' moments which brought us joy or happiness, a sense of achievement or an occasion calling for celebration (s) etc. While every day may not be as eventful, it is upon us to create 'Cheerful' moments. A simple greeting every morning and night accompanied with a hug can create a 'Cheerful' moment. The second set would be the 'Dismal' moments i.e., the not-so-cheerful, sad moments which disappoint, discourage and bring sorrow or pain. Again, it was upon us to figure out moments and incidents that translated into 'Dismal' moments. The third set was 'Taken for granted' moments akin to a trashcan where all the ignored moments get collected. These often contain the once 'Cheerful' or 'Dismal' moments that we take for granted. The third set usually contains the most number of moments. Keeping tabs on any or all of these moments did not require elaborate calculations or housekeeping. All that was needed was to be conscious of our behavior.

Viewing daily activities in terms of these moments often resulted in a mix of both 'Cheerful' and 'Dismal' moments. A person with a positive outlook would most likely see an almost equal proportion of both 'Cheerful' and 'Dismal' moments. Such people tend to draw energy from the 'Cheerful' moments. The 'Dismal' moments while bothersome quickly get converted into the 'Taken for granted' moments. On the other hand, one with a negative outlook would most likely prolong the 'Dismal moments'. The 'Cheerful' moments are often nothing more than in-transit 'Taken for granted' moments.

Moments, whether 'Cheerful' or 'Dismal' tend to be relative and thus differ from person to person. For a daily wager, serving meals to the family is a 'Cheerful' moment. In comparison, to a well-settled family, daily meals are hardly anything worth being 'Cheerful' about. It is thus a 'Taken for granted' moment. The same family when occasionally dining out treats it as a 'Cheerful' moment. Done frequently, the once 'Cheerful' moment now becomes a 'Taken for granted' moment.

While perceiving to be positive, we missed noticing what our actions depicted. Irrespective of our outlook, we gathered lots of 'Taken for granted' moments. The key to maintaining a positive attitude was instead to gather lots of 'Cheerful' moments and reduce the 'Dismal' and 'Taken for granted' moments.

Developing an understanding brought us insight into our parenting style. Just as 'Cheerful' and 'Dismal' moments affected us, so too were they affecting our children. We quite likely were the source of most of it. Here then was an opportunity to increase the number of 'Cheerful' moments and reduce the 'Dismal' moments that originated from us.

A question as simple as "How often did we encourage or appreciate our child?" helped bring about the desired change. Our children, like most individuals enjoy being appreciated and encouraged and it is something they expected of us. I remember encouraging and appreciating them when they were toddlers. Growing up, something seems to have transpired which took away the 'Cheerful' moments resulting from my appreciation. This "something" was my taking for granted most of their 'Cheerful' moments. Having realized my oversight, small changes in my behavior triggered a jump in their 'Cheerful' moments!

As for the "Dismal moments", gathering and grouping helped eliminate redundancy and avoiding discussions in the heat of the moment. It also gave us time to rethink on the areas to be addressed. We also filtered the list by picking the top item and reaching out to children during their receptive moments. Grabbing them during their receptive moments and twining it to their learning style made better impact. The elder one is more receptive during an evening walk while the younger one prefers to hear it in the form of a story, emotional and sentimental. The goal was to put a positive spin.

I don't think we followed everything to the tee; instead, we went with the thought behind it. Getting down to basics you realize not everything will suit your need. The key then is to figure out what helps bring about a positive outlook. For us, what started with the creation a positive environment continued with identification of "moments". I believe irrespective of age, individuals with a positive attitude are more likely to accept themselves.

Embracing the Gift of Challenges

'The struggle you're in today is developing the strength you need for tomorrow. Don't give up.' ~ **Robert Tew**

The word challenge evokes multiple meanings; for discussion in this section, it can be explained as a task or situation that tests one's ability. Even in my family, a challenge was never considered a good thing. They were always undesirable, be it their timings or associated element of luck. In reality, it does not always mean to cause trouble; instead, it often carries opportunity enveloped within. Opportunity and challenge are two sides of the same coin. Viewing the opportunity required me to look past the challenges, whether at home or work. Most people I encountered got caught up worrying about the challenge, missing out on the opportunity knocking their door.

Understanding how we deal with challenges is nothing short of confusing. If one were to draw conclusions watching people drive on the wrong side of the road, violate traffic lights, jumping queues etc., it can easily be perceived that we love challenges, the types which give an easy way out. The same can also be ascertained watching people work their way, through government offices, school/college admissions etc.

While taking the easy way out may seem natural, it is starting to become a systemic problem. A couple of years ago my elder child approached me asking, 'I want to be rich, which career would be right?'. I went through a bunch of emotions in the next few seconds. I was dumbstruck and annoyed at her question. Feeling disappointed for not inculcating the right values and yet pretending to be calm, I silently took some deep breaths. With a frown, I responded of not knowing any formula that made people rich. What I knew was that people didn't just become rich, instead it was a side effect of something they did really well, such as being passionate, doing what they believe in and which interests them. Digging into each of the aspects, I explained how when people do things well, it helps differentiate them from the rest and that is what brings in the money. While the discussion ended, my reflection continued….'Did I fail to make them realize the gift of embracing challenges?'

Dr. Shreeram Geet - These days majority of youngsters when looking for careers first ask about the pay package. Attractions have reoriented with package attraction becoming a systemic issue. People do not come with aspirations; instead, it is the pay package which decides their aspirations. At certain level all packages look attractive. It is when the real difficulty starts, that such an approach develops into a sidelined career.

As a child, I probably didn't perceive challenges any differently. Things I enjoyed were often done right; dealing with the rest was often a formality. It was not until my early twenties that I learnt to see the opportunity enveloped within challenges. Not all challenges were worth chasing, but picking the right one required rationale. While on the one hand, I wanted to brief them and coach them to embrace challenges head-on, on the other I wanted them to independently develop an understanding. Assuaging my concerns of them not doing things right, I tried to remember my own self at that age.

Wondering, if not the frequent encounters, what would help embrace challenges? Everybody has their fair share and yet we do not particularly have a liking for them. Ideally, shouldn't we develop a better understanding of something so common? What could be the rationale behind our resistance? Challenges big or small have an element of risk associated. Coupled with this its disruptive nature of popping up anywhere and breaking one's rhythm thus leading to anxiety makes it is all-the-more unwelcome. That said, could the prime reason be the manner in which one goes about addressing a challenge?

My instinct to look for an easier solution often implied not understanding the root cause. Whenever I took the efforts to understand, it ushered learning and a pleasurable experience. Challenges seem to be packed with learning, associated either with the individual, situation or surroundings. One's inability to associate learning with challenges could be the probable reason to view them as a distraction and thus the resistance.

Though individual instances might not qualify, they do act as building blocks in knowing how one deal with challenges. The tendency of taking the easier route is likely to form a pattern getting replicated elsewhere in day-to-day lives. Whether it is dealing with one's career or children, preference for immediate result might imply taking less challenging approaches.

Keen on understanding it from a parenting standpoint, I grouped challenges into two kinds, immediate and gradual.

- **Immediate Challenges** - These do not present much of a choice and have to be faced head-on as and when they crop up. These are more in-your-face kinds, are relatively smaller and carry lower risks. Some examples of these could be like getting children's workbooks completed, completing homework etc.

- **Gradual Challenges** - These are not the in-your-face kinds and hence difficult to identify immediately. Locating these calls for a degree of keenness and farsightedness whereas addressing them calls for planning and time. The long-term risks associated with these challenges are also larger. However, given their non-disruptive nature, they tend to get pushed under other immediate challenges and in most cases never get addressed. Examples of these include developing a child's interest in education, creating a sense of ownership, overcoming their fear of failure, inculcating values etc.

Unlike immediate challenges, the gradual ones require special attention given that it pays dividends in the long run. Children like adults are also likely to develop the habit of evading them. Given its long-term benefits, coaching may be required to view them positively.

Drawing analogies from the corporate world, I used to wonder why most offices have mockup fire drills at regular intervals. I realized their worth later. These are like preparing for a gradual challenge compared to a fire suddenly breaking out, an immediate challenge. For some, it may seem a waste of time going up and down stairs and setting ears ringing to the sound of alarms. These though have a serious purpose behind them, the first and foremost being a check on the level of preparedness to handle a fatal situation, followed by an understanding of the degree to which volunteers know their roles and the condition of essential equipment(s). Besides, it helps identify gaps in planning and gets every individual on the premises to know what is expected of them as also accustom them to a real-life situation.

In short, the mock up drill prepares people for a potential challenge by rehearsing and thus avoid panic when the situation presents itself. This also helps bring in the "been there done that" feeling. When people are prepared and know what they need to do, they also feel in control thus making it easier to deal with challenges.

I am often at loggerheads with children while persuading them to embrace gradual challenges. Activities that require long term planning and commitment never make it to the children to-do lists. Seeing values in such activities require foresight or long-term perspective. The ability to see beyond seems to come with maturity. Children with their short-term perspective are likely to not understand parents' viewpoints that are based on long-term perspectives and vice-versa. The lack of urgency while dealing with gradual challenges means one can afford the opportunity to make mistakes and learn from them.

Thereafter, when exposed to challenges on a regular basis, children realize that these are no big deal.

While most of us adults overcome challenges on a daily basis, we reflect very little on the learning. Coaching children to reflect on the cause and effect can mean takeaways that are good for life. A simple exercise of identifying things that went well and those that could be done better helps the child associate challenges with learning. In addition to being prepared to face similar challenges, it shatters any fear that exists in their minds about dealing with challenges. They thus learn to see both sides of the coin.

I believe those who fear challenges are the ones bound to face them the most. Anything that causes them to stretch their abilities may seem like a challenge irrespective of the level of hardship involved. Conversely, those comfortable dealing with them may not even realize their presence. They are most likely to make a difference by constantly overcoming and thriving on them and shall lead lives relatively challenge-free.

Challenges big or small have a shelf life, in other words they come with an expiry date. They hate to live forever and despise making friends. When faced with one, the obvious reaction for most is "why me" realizing little that nobody is free of challenges. What varies though is how one perceives them and the steps taken to overcome them. Activities such as cooking or driving can be very stressful for some though relaxing for others. This difference in approach largely depends upon how a challenge is addressed. While challenges are common, there should never be a need to hunt for more. Simply, the effort you put in addressing it should be worth the learning.

In some ways, opportunity is what we make out of an uncomfortable situation. Truth is, challenges are part of life and one cannot run away from it all the time. It is equally true that every individual learns to deal with them in their own way. As parents we ought to see them as hidden opportunities to coach our progeny to embrace them early in life. Such exposure will not only help children learn from experiences but also help them realize the ingredients of their own recipe.

Children who are adept at embracing challenges should be made aware of their strength. The focus for such children can be to get things done right. This implies focusing on 'how one overcomes a challenge'.

Overcoming the Fear of Failure

'The greatest glory in living lies not in never falling, but in rising every time we fall.' ~ **Nelson Mandela**

The thought of 'Am I setting my wards up for failure' often challenged my parenting practices. It was easy to do more, decide for them, get involved in everything they do, etc. What was difficult was pulling back, giving them a free hand and letting them explore. Fear of failure as I experienced as a parent had two aspects a) Parents' fear of their children failing and, b) Children's fear of failure.

Parents' fear of their children failing - I was so paranoid of my children failing that I would try and set goals in everything they did. Even simple card games such as UNO were not overlooked. Though being able to visualize the big picture was my strength, I missed it when it came to my children. Coaching them to differentiate in everything they did be it karate, drawing or academics, often ended squeezing the fun element out of it. I was successfully transmitting my fear of being measured as a parent. Parent's fear of their children failing, in other words could be described as children not living up to parent's expectation.

An interesting incident happened that reminded me of the pitfalls of ever safeguarding. We have a Caribbean trumpet tree, in front of our house. When in bloom, its leaves gave way to the bright yellow flowers that draw different kind of sunbirds and bees. As a sapling, it needed frequent care and support. Growing, it had difficulty supporting its own weight, especially during monsoon when we would reinforce its supports. Years passed and I kept providing it support never once realizing that the plant had grown into a tree. During the monsoon of 2014, I missed reinforcing it, and unable to bear its own weight, the tree finally stooped all the way to the floor. The only option to save the tree was to cut it off from where it bent. Disturbed by the incident, I deliberated on whether our effort for the tree over the years was correct or not. Knowing fully well that the tree was unable to carry its weight, we kept supporting it until the time it came crashing down. Unsure if by supporting, I had improved its chances or reduced its chances of survival. What if I had stopped supporting it earlier? Would it have fallen and broken? Even if it had, would a smaller fall be easier to overcome than its current state.

Looking around, I find many instances where smaller failures were safeguarded setting the stage for bigger ones. I could also relate it to my uncle who went almost bankrupt on three occasions due to his penchant for the tipple. On each occasion, his brothers upon the insistence of their mother rescued him but all being in vain. Fed up, they left him to his ways. Looking back, I wonder who was at fault, my uncle himself, his upbringing or his surrounding. Were not the rescue attempts in some way setting him up for a bigger failure?

Was I in some ways also mimicking a similar behavior with my children? My well- intentioned handholding and helping may avert smaller failures initially but might be setting them up for bigger failures. Whether it was taking the easy way out or not putting their best effort, it had little to do with my children and was in fact a fear embedded in me. Younger children seem to have little fear unequipped as they are to think about the consequences. They end up doing an excellent job at absorbing parents' fears. This fear grows proportionately with age and becomes a permanent feature.

Bhooshan Shukla - It is true that parents go overboard and handicap children. Children need to experiment, fail, get in trouble and learn to get out of trouble. Often giving them freedom to experiment implies shielding the younger generation from the older generation.

Children need help and it is the parents' responsibility to provide assistance. The question is for how long. Do parents have to wait till the child starts to own the problems? Most parents take it to be their life's purpose to help their offspring. Carried away, they stop at nothing, providing them with crutches and hoping things will sort out with time. Parents helping children and owning their problem is like taking control of the reins. I noticed, owning their problems caused them to take a back seat and get further distanced. It also implies the inability of connecting consequences to their actions. Any failure or gaps automatically get associated with the owner, and children not being the owners, learn little from these experiences. Despite realizing that almost everybody fails at more than one occasion in life, either as a child, a parent, in marriage or at work, I seemed reluctant to coach and make children understand its significance. Could it be that, I underestimated the importance of overcoming the fear of failure and realizing that failure is just a step towards reaching the goal?

Children's fear of failure- Failure as I describe in regards to an individual can be another opportunity to learn'. Unlike the other attributes, fear of failure brings with it the good, the bad and the ugly aspects. The good that fear brings is the motivation it provides to achieve if not overachieve a goal. The bad is that it can make people nervous or unexcited causing them to lose interest and not pursue goals. Afraid of being labeled a looser they instead prefer to not try. The ugly is the 'don't care' attitude. Latching on makes one insensitive to fear or its consequences. Just imagine all the great inventors being overcome by the fear of failure! We wouldn't have moved beyond the stone-age!

Dr. Shreeram Geet - Failure is an essential part of life, the more you fail, the more you rise. Children of parents who encourage them despite failures while making them understand it to be a natural process, invariably excel in life. You have to understand the reason for failure and go on compensating for it.

My kids exhibited different reactions based on situations. In areas of interest/ comfort, fear often worked as a motivator; it was as if their reputation or pride was at stake. In other areas, the thought of failing often restrained them from even attempting. It induced a kind of fear that was not willingly accepted and the option often exercised was giving up. While at times, reinforcements in the form of reflecting on some of their past triumphs helped, they often needed confidence boosters. There was also the display of a care-a-damn kind of an attitude. Here nothing mattered; neither pride nor highlighting the consequences had any impact. Intimidation was nothing but bad ploy.

Being a parent, the display of lack of anxiety by children was hard to digest; It was their absolute confidence though that left me puzzled. While my usual reaction was to unsettle them, it was not until later that I realized to view calmness as their strength. Mostly it is our worries of the consequences that puts fear in our mind. These fears are like transparent walls that influences and limit ones ability. Those who exhibit a "don't care a damn" attitude hardly put up such walls; in other words they exhibit no limits. The fact that they were unlike me didn't mean they were wrong.

I recollect Rashi, all of 16 then, despite being independent, courageous and a quick learner going through patches of low confidence. Noticing her withdraw, I could make out that there was more to it than was visible. Digging into some of her recent capers revealed a pattern. She avoided participating in debates at school, traded the key role in her school play, did not seem very excited to fill in for her karate classes and did not enjoy writing a book review. This, along with her actions looked like she was avoiding exposure, which seemed to bother her as well. A few casual conversations later, I confronted her with the pattern and she confessed. Taking this as an opportunity, I explained to her how life's highs and lows affected everybody and facing up to them was the only solution. It is how one deals with these moments that defines one's character. Such situations in essence help one identify the ingredients of their recipe. Encouraging her to look at things as a whole, I pitched on her being talented and gifted, and that by circumventing challenges she was only missing out on opportunities which are a way of knowing oneself.

When depressed, a quick way to motivate one-self would be to look into the past and ask pertinent questions like 'how often have I failed'. A simple question such as this can help regain one's confidence. In reality, failures are rare; it happens only when one chooses not to learn. Anything that offers learning in exchange can hardly be considered a failure. I also made her do certain exercises, like jotting down her strengths and areas of improvement besides identifying all kinds of wins in the last 6 months. Doing so helps as at times one's perception of self deviates dramatically from reality, which was the case with our daughter. The exercise with all its facts in place helped her regain her lost confidence. Coincidentally, a week later her English teacher asked her to present on the topic 'Fear of Failure'!

It also reminded me of my nephew's courageous stand. Struggling with his minimal interest in education, his parents kept nudging him to explore other interests as well. Couple of years down the road, they arrived at a crossroad. Worried that their nudging may do no good and set him up for bigger failure, they collectively decide to take a break from school. Schools however may not be supportive of such thoughts.

One such learning that I often endorse is 'failing' is not bad and in fact failing sooner is better than later. Failure played a pivotal role in shaping me as an individual. Failing early on in a way resembled getting early feedback, a blessing. It helps minimize impact, save time and cost. It is interesting to see the effect of early feedback on the automotive industry which spends big sums in elaborate design, building prototype etc. Doing so helps them minimize shocks, maximize early feedback and reduced chances of failure later. A similar approach augurs well with individuals as well. The sooner children learn to overcome their fear of failure the more eventful life becomes in the long run.

While we made a conscious attempt to avoid setting them up for failure, commitments from their side mandated different treatment. When it came to commitments, we rarely let them off the hook. A commitment, once made by them had to be followed through.

Whether it was my fear of the children failing or their fear of failing, the best means to coach them was to let them experience it all first-hand. The goal was to make them independent and drive-in the point that failure was not the end; instead it is just a milestone closer to the goal. What good would it do to limit them from exercising their curiosity or their ability to experiment?

There was no point in clipping their wings and expecting them to fly when they grew.

How fast children adapt to situations depends on the number of supports provided to them. Those too dependent on parents to accomplish things may choose to go slow and work towards withdrawing these supports one at a time. Children like everyone are bound to make mistakes and stumble; there should be nothing earth shattering about this. Let them fail early on and succeed when it matters.

Having a Purpose

'Purpose is what gives life its meaning' ~ **C. H. Parkhurst**

Generations have collectively set out to overcome challenges that have been unique to them. Transition from joint to nuclear families was fueled probably by urbanization; similarly, the surge in middle-class spending was in all probability ignited by an urge for education. Expressed differently, preceding generation(s) act as enablers for the succeeding ones. The challenges encountered, big or small had some aspects in common; they brought desire, commitment and the most crucial ingredient of them all, immediate goals. The last one came in the form of dwelling in the city, taking care of the elderly, providing for the family, buying a house etc.

Not too long ago, as a current generation parent with most of my immediate goals secured, I wondered what would be next for my children. Would priorities of the preceding generation such as the aim to become an Engineer or Doctor be the way or would a stable government job do the trick? One thing was certain though; unlike the previous generations, the future one would most likely be void of immediate goals.

With a foundation in place and a mind set free, what then will help them find that inner peace, think big, fly high and make a global impact? Would the challenge for the current generation of parents be, how to prepare their children for flight?

A seemingly unconvinced Anita was curious to know why challenges of the prior generations were not relevant any longer. When probed on her childhood aspiration, what came across were objectives such as a house in the city and a car. When probed on our children's likely aspirations, all she heard of was that they wanted to make money. In a certain way, it emphasized my point. The prior generations had goals that were immediate in nature and somewhat in-your-face. Moreover, these were common and so were the means to achieve them. The good thing about them was that they bound you and provided a sense of direction. Distractions find them difficult to dethrone, and until achieved, remain the sole purpose in your life.

Dr. Yajyoti Singh - Financial security has helped children choose the careers they want. They are explicit in their knowledge about where they are headed and time it shall take. They are in a way spoilt by choice, but confident and not scared of changing goals. They are also more cognitively exposed to what they can do later in life.

Immediate goals have no relevance to today's younger generation who cannot relate to the same feeling of rush. They would rather take longer and be different. What they have is a much bigger canvas where they can leave behind their impressions. One such way is to develop a strong sense of purpose which indicates a higher calling; a calling to give back to the world more than if not equal to what one has received and try and make it a better place. 'The point is that purpose is about more than just ourselves - it's also about having a positive impact on the lives of others in some way.' ([5]http://www.handsonscotland.co.uk)

The sense of purpose is like a guiding star that makes the journey of life enriching and satisfying. It helps align one's energy and actions so as to achieve a cause that one cares about and relates to strongly.

---

[5] "Sense of Purpose", http://www.handsonscotland.co.uk/flourishing_and_wellbeing_in_children_and_young_people/flourishing_topic_frameset.htm (collected 17 Dec 2015)

Dr. Bhooshan Shukla - Having a purpose in life is a very adult feeling that children are unlikely to understand and relate to. In fact few adults get it and it is unfair to expect the same from children. Being concepts of a higher order, these could end-up distancing the child. It comes to those who understand the sense of purpose and need not be guided by others. Awareness itself is a process and nobody knows when it will happen.

Sharing the same with Anita, I insisted on explaining how it differed from a goal. Having a purpose and working towards it, is different from working towards a goal. Working towards a purpose may mean overcoming multiple goals on its way. Purpose is something that one believes in, it never ceases to exist. Goals are finite; you achieve and move towards the next. An example of a goal could be to become a doctor and an example of a purpose could be to 'Help eliminate child mortality'. A purpose could be associated to anything, art, music, history, environment, surrounding, welfare of underprivileged etc.

A purpose cannot be created it has to come from within. One's purpose is a mixture of multiple things, personality, passion, exposure and values. When all these factors coincide, it gives rise to a purpose that is strong and something you believe in for life. Purpose is neither big nor small, nor is it geeky or fancy. A purpose is where one puts his/ her heart into achieving something, and everybody around helps them live that purpose. People who have a purpose have it wired into them; they wake up inspired wanting to live their purpose. Their drive is so focused that all challenges on the way look smaller and immaterial.

Explaining this to my daughter Rashi of 16 then ended on a sour note. The intention was to have her pursue a career in areas she cares. She found it difficult to relate, as she did not know what she was passionate about or what she valued most. I guess it is a bit like the chicken and egg situation. Knowing what one is passionate about requires some amount of exposure and experience. Lack of these make everything appear rosy on the surface; it is only when you get into its underpinning that its essence gets exposed.

She began her career search wanting to become a fashion designer. Not the creative kind, upon gathering information about the industry, challenges, lifestyle and watching documentaries she realized this was not her calling and changed her mind. Some months later, becoming an obstetrician fancied her. While the subject continues to interests her, the fear of not getting selected seemed to dissuade her. My role was to guide them to learn about themselves; their values and passion would likely follow.

Dr. Shreeram Geet - Purpose is everywhere though very few find it. One in ten thousand finds it early with one in a thousand finding it around the age of 35 and many never until retirement. It is not careers but purpose that brings in satisfaction and while it is important to know it, identifying it is far from easy. If you take writers of classic literature as an example, most find their purpose around the age of 35.

I never thought of age being a factor in finding ones purpose. For me, anytime is good time to find ones purpose in life. I only found mine recently. It is not necessary that everybody finds theirs. Some may find it early, some late and some never. There are also those who do not feel the need to have a purpose or goals, and yet are content in their own ways. Purpose and goals provide a method to structure the madness around one. It helps focus on priorities and achieve things that matter. It is about having that little fire named desire burning within, emitting light and helping one find one's objective.

Dr. Bhooshan Shukla - Children have one ingredient in abundance, hope. It is what keeps them going; they are always hopeful and that is good enough. Our job is to keep their hopes alive. If as parents, one cannot trust their children's ability, how can one expect the children to trust their own abilities? Children question their trustworthiness if they sense parents who are generally blinded to children faults having difficulty trusting them.

Having a purpose may seem like wishful thinking though it is exactly what the future generations needs. They do not need goals that they cannot relate to; instead, what they need is something that will inspire them and they can associate with. Having laid the foundation, parents are then not too far in helping their children realize this. All they need hence is guidance that helps them prepare and take off.

The Gist

The topics in this part are nothing that children cannot overcome in their adult life. Instead, the aim is to broaden their horizon and help them blossom in the best possible way.

Although, not the kind who over-comforted the children, I was certainly at fault when it came to too much intervention. I had difficulty seeing them as individuals and instead saw them as my extension. While I did well providing them with exposure, they had little realization of their behavior. Often their preferences were not a result of having tried out different options; it was instead driven by their desire not to try.

As parents, getting into the children's shoes was not easy, never-the-less, it is an ongoing experience. It helped me become less moody and inconsistent, and a lot more appreciative. In attempting to maintain a positive environment at home, we learnt to have conversations that were constructive besides learning to backout when it headed nowhere. We also managed to track and monitor our own behavior in regards to 'Cheerful' and 'Dismal' moments.

Challenges do not discriminate though realizing this fact was far from easy. Preference for the easy path had seeped into our children as well. Wanting to become rich, they wanted to know which careers to choose. Understanding challenges and realizing that they too have a shelf life helped group them into 'immediate' and 'gradual'. While the 'immediate' ones demand attention, the 'gradual' ones carry the potential to make a difference though over time.

Presenting the children with crutches was easy, letting them stumble difficult. In my case, it was more to do with my fear of them failing which made it difficult pulling back and giving them a free hand. Failing is not bad but setting them up for it is. These early stumbles help children prepare for the long run and overcome their fear of failure.

The lack of immediate goals and too many options to choose from is not necessarily a bad thing. It is just that finding the right alignment might take time. For this, they need a much bigger canvas and along with it, time and trust. Unaware that having a purpose may be more of an adult feeling, I pushed it through making things turn sour.

An exercise on 'Growth Beyond the Comfort Zone'

Pitfalls of the "Comfort Zone"

a) Are your child's preferences a result of having tried out different things?

b) How willing are they to gather experiences, try out different things, go to different places etc.?

c) Do you see children as your extension?

d) How much of your likes/ dislikes do you impose on your children?

e) How independent are your children in doing their activity?

f) Do you prefer to go with the flow or do you believe in nurturing children such that stumbling early may help them run when it matters?

g) Have you come across children playing mind games to get their demands fulfilled?

Maintaining a Positive Outlook

h) What techniques do you use to maintaining a positive outlook?

i) How do you respond to criticism from children?

j) From where do you draw energy?

k) What does your daily activity showcase: 'Cheerful' or 'Dismal' moments?

Embracing the Gift of Challenges

l) Do you prefer doing things right or taking the easy way out?

m) How do you view challenges?

n) How much effort do you put in addressing the gradual kind of challenges?

Overcoming the Fear Of Failure

o) Do you worry about setting your wards up for failure?

p) Are you children provided with crutches?

q) Do you think it is better to fail early than late?

r) How much time, if any, do you spend in accumulating learning from you failures?

s) Do you fear for your children? Is it seeded by your fear of the children failing or the children's fear of failure?

Having a Purpose

t) Do you believe in the rationale of having a purpose?

u) Do your children have the freedom to pursue what they believe in?

CHAPTER

5

Relaying Values

'Keep your values positive because your values become your destiny.' **~ Mahatma Gandhi**

It is ironic that values despite being at the core of everything one does, is seldom nurtured. I love introspecting and yet my values stayed hidden until I was in my mid thirties. I am unsure if my father knew his values; he never spoke of them. Yet, he lived and breathed them. He was not a perfect individual by any means, but he was consistent.

There was never a sermon on what values to nurture and yet we siblings read him alike. I wondered how he messaged; it must have been embedded in his actions. It is thus for parents to decide which family values they intend to pass down to the next generation. Here are some that I believe are relevant for future generation.

Bhooshan Shukla - Inculcating values is not about being philosophical; it is instead all about action. Unfortunately, parenting in India is mostly about preaching, pampering and lacking relevant action. Criticize our European counterparts all we like, but got to give it to them for being hands-on parents.

Significance of Values

'It's not hard to make decisions once you know what your values are' ~ **Roy E. Disney**

Values are beliefs that matter to an individual. They can be grouped into 5 different areas, personal, family, socio-cultural, material, spiritual and moral values. ([6]Juan Carlos Jimenez)

Personal values while unique to an individual are often embedded through one's upbringing, environment, education and experience. They also help comprehend what one considered acceptable or unacceptable behavior. The rationale behind one's behavior is often hidden deep below in their values.

Once learnt, it was hard not noticing it in everything I did. Interestingly, my siblings remember witnessing it in my behavior right from childhood. While few of my values have changed over the years, parenting has certainly made me aware and consistent.

Values have been around since ancient times, relayed as part of one's upbringing and teachings. They were ingrained in how people conducted themselves, often taking the form of family values. During the predominance of joint families, inculcating family values may not have been a rigorous affair, yet abundant opportunities existed for children to learn. The fact that families took pride in their values may have made comprehending easier for the young. The advent of nuclear families may have altered the trend, but the legacy continues. On the surface it may seem like instilling values has lost its emphasis, but that might not be true.

Growing up in a nuclear family, there was a conscious attempt to teach what was considered correct and incorrect behavior though never was it approached from a value standpoint. As a result, though values were ingrained in how I behaved, it took effort to understand them.

---

[6] Juan Carlos Jimenez, "Types of values", http://significanceofvalues.com/

I remember taxing my brand new sedan on the busy streets of Pune finding parking space. The spot we finally found was objected by an old woman peeping out of her shop perched on stilts. Ignoring the grumpy woman, I parked having taken long to find a spot and was certain of not blocking the path to her shop. Upon our arrival 30 minutes later, Anita noticed a foot long line deeply etched on the front passenger door. Unsure of how to vent my anger, I asked the woman if it made her happy and drove back home. For the next two days, I felt torn apart acting like a cowherd on the one hand and a fool on the other. Unsure of how to calm down, my values came to my rescue. It not only left me feeling right choosing not to retaliate but also made me content with who I was.

Dr. Shreeram Geet – Most people are unaware of their values. For a family person, values are rarely a personal decision. Knowing one's values and living by them are two different things. Living one's values requires them to be shared with the family and supported by all.

Sharing with my family the exercise on values I implemented at work, opened up questions from my elder child, Rashi. The idea was to garner their support and help in being consistent. She was keen on knowing how values influenced ones behavior. Illustrating it, I targeted integrity as one of the probable values. If 'Honoring Integrity' is a value that matters, one's behaviors need to exhibit the same. This implies being honest, ethical and standing by one's word in every aspect of life. Whether it is at work, at home or in public, values need nurturing and thus living by them. While they tend to evolve over time with knowledge and exposure, living by one's values is not always easy. Even those who know their values, struggle to bridge the gap between what they value and the behavior they exhibit. Knowing one's values and reflecting on the behaviors exhibited helps bridge potential gaps.

Mulling over it, she seemed keen on knowing how values differed from one's recipe. Values ought to be different from one's recipe, I exclaimed. Values are things one believes in, which one considers acceptable or unacceptable behavior. Values of the personal types are mostly positive in nature and there exist no such thing as right or wrong values. Ordered in priority, they are generally verbs denoting an action. E.g. Honesty – Be truthful, Diversity – Embrace all religions, Compassionate – Sympathize with others etc.

A recipe on the other hand consists of adjectives, which describes the person and gives insight into one's characteristics such as, passion, strengths, weaknesses, priorities, personality etc. They consist of both positive and negative attributes. Most importantly, these ingredients are proof of the behaviors the person exhibits. The numbers of attributes one can have are not limited in an individual recipe as opposed to personal values which are usually in single digits.

Values are a way of looking at an individual from inside-out identifying one's beliefs and thus behaving accordingly. A recipe looks at things outside-in identifying attributes by looking at one's behavior. Identifying the values that matter to an individual helps align one's career, relationship or conduct with children.

Mentioned below are some simpler family values that I found relevant for my children. These were used to introduce them to and develop their foundation of values.

Being thankful for what one has

'Never let the things you want make you forget the things you have.' ~ ***Anonymous***

When my children were toddlers, I often played a game of swapping roles. They would be the nutty parent and I would be their loving child. Mimicking them, I used it to mock things such as their candy crazy behavior. They would do their best to pacify the child in me, often acting just the opposite of what I did as a parent. The play would eventually end with them putting their foot down on how things will be. It often resulted in us bursting out laughing. Deep inside, my teaching often resulted in learning.

Now grown up, wanting pretty much everything that catches their fancy and as impulsively, I wonder if the ploys have reversed. It took me a while realizing that the only consistent outcome was my frustration. Looking for opportunities to better, the simplest of disputes threw me in circles. Difficult to please, I took pride in finding faults. With frustration peaking, the only escape route was channelizing it into something soothing such as 'Being Thankful'. Knowing that every child has something to offer had a calming effect. If nothing else, children staying healthy means so much to parents, yet we take things for granted constantly asking for more. Children have so many little things to offer, should being off-track in a few areas really matter? In other words, better or worse is nothing but perspective. No matter how bad the situation, one can still find ways to feel better. Regretting my behavior and bringing about the desired change was not instantaneous and neither was it sticky. Confessing to the kids and Anita helped in adapting to the change.

While prevalent across generations, not appreciating what one has seems amplified in the younger generation. Sheltered from the harsh realities of life, they seem rarely gratified for what they have. Instead, it is always about things they do not possess or taking others for granted. The desire to own it all has little to do with their likings and seems more of an obsession. In some ways, these children live in a bubble, having difficulty comprehending the hardship and sacrifices their parents go through.

Being thankful, as I understand is about appreciating the simple things in life and thanking those who make it happen. I found it easy to comprehend when broken down into needs and wants. As I understand, 'needs' are things that one has to have i.e. the basics, while 'wants' are things that one would like to have. While I knew it for long, I never attempted putting it to practical use. Though not apt, the example I quote here is closest to heart. I was a kind of automotive junkie who fancied cars right from the 70s Stingray to the Soft-tail Choppers. Not that I could afford them, but my hobby had turned into an obsession. So much so that eating or drinking inside the family car was forbidden; even getting in without dusting one's feet was unwelcome. Getting over this materialistic obsession required continuous reminder that the car was far from being a need, and it was there to serve the family instead of the family serving the car. Though simple and unconvincing as it may seem, the concept of needs and wants can be applied to pretty much everything.

My children were no different; they were far from realizing that their attempts at finding happiness in materialistic things were fleeting. Their concept of 'needs' and 'wants' were thoroughly mixed-up; all they had was one big bucket of 'needs', with no notion of 'wants'.

In other words, they thought of 'wants' as being their right with ever-newer ones replacing those fulfilled. They often went to great lengths pressing for their 'wants' and at times creating uncomfortable situations for both. When unable to get their demands fulfilled, they did an excellent job at making us feel guilty. Unsure if such behaviors could have ramifications such as acceptance of family members, fostering negativity etc., we had to find a way out. In an extreme sense, the inability to curb their obsession could also make them easy targets for wrong doings.

Dr. Yajyoti Singh - Sensitizing children on the basics of needs and wants is part of parenting. Over-indulgence causes the thin line between needs and wants to disappear. They then do not want things, they just need them. They need to be told that asking for something time and again does not imply being provided the same.

It is quite likely that the future generation(s) may never experience the kind of hardships, the earlier ones did. They still ought to be aware of the difference between needs and wants. Developing an understanding not only helps in being thankful for what one has but also helps avoid taking things for granted. In addition, it also curtails negativity. Children need to know that none get everything in life. Even those who can afford it all, end up trading it with their privacy and freedom. Although, comparisons of any kind are not ideal, children worrying about their 'wants' should feel privileged of their 'needs' being addressed.

Dr. Bhooshan Shukla - While difference between needs and wants is a good thing for children to learn, they are not for younger children and are rather tricky a discussion to have with older ones. The feeling of being deprived is constant in most children irrespective of who their parents. It is important to be realistic and lead by action.

Explaining it, Rushil popped the question 'You mean one should be content with what one has?' I responded with a long 'no'. Being thankful is not the same as being content or not being ambitious. It does not imply compromising; instead, it implies being grounded. One can certainly expect more from oneself and one's parents, but not without appreciating what one already possesses. I illustrated this by highlighting the self-inflicted problem we had created at home by introducing the kids to varied cuisines. It has boomeranged on us in that they now expected such food to be served to them- round the clock! Simple Indian food often became a source of annoyance turning dinnertime, synonymous with family time which now resembled battle time!

Finding recourse in the concept of needs versus wants, I elaborated further that placing food on the table was primary, a need compared to things such as cuisines, repetitiveness, etc. which are secondary i.e. a want. A lot of efforts go into putting food on the table. Criticizing comes easy compared to appreciation. Special requests for food at home cannot be addressed at the last minute unlike restaurants, which are primarily meant for just that. These can always be entertained, provided they are intimated in time. In this case, it is not about being content but instead about being proactive and thankful.

Just hearing about a concept has never been adequate for me and so is the case with the kids. Following it up with an exercise helps it register firmly. An exercise requiring them to list their 'needs' and 'wants' helped in understanding the difference between the two. Having them prioritize their 'wants' was easy, discussing the 'needs' and building consensus was another battle. Once there was enough clarity on the concept of priority, I took it a step further by providing them the means to earn their wants. This is explained in the section "Earning it".

With the reality that their 'wants' change often, having them do the exercises every time it changes was a sure recipe for disaster. One remedy though was to introduce them to the concept of earning their 'wants'.

Children, like the rest of us embrace certain practices and drop the others which end-up creating hurdles for us as parents. With the exercises I introduced my children into, this has reduced though not eliminated in entirety. There is a better understanding now of why all 'wants' may not be met. While one has embraced it more, the other has earned lot more 'wants'.

Earning it

'There are three ingredients in the good life; learning, earning and yearning.'~ **Christopher Morley**

Given the controversial nature of the topic, I will attempt presenting it as it transpired. My experience over the years has shown that every aspect of parenting has its pros and cons; a sort of a balancing act, the same can be said of children earning their 'wants'. While I am in favor of inculcating the habit early on, the need arose specifically due to two reasons; the first providing children a means to earn their 'wants', the second, developing in them, an interest for physical activities.

Dr. Bhooshan Shukla - Fundamentally, I believe whatever household chores one does in the family should not be monetized in any way, tangible or intangible. Because, that is exactly what family is about. Even at work, not everything that one does gets translated into salary, hike or promotion. We do lot of things because the situation demands so.

Family outings to a mall or even a visit to the grocery store close-by with elementary-school-age children was a challenge. It mostly ended in displeasure for all. Irrespective of the preparedness or warning, one glimpse of something they liked was enough for them to go berserk. It is hard describing it. Was it their inability to contain their excitement, the greed to have it all, lack of frequent visit to the mall or part and parcel of parents' shopping experience? Irrespective of these, our outings mostly ended in displeasure for both children and us. Their constant haggling necessitated the need to do something different. Thus was born a point system that equated into token money meant to provide them the means to procure stuff they desired without our intervention. This took care of the embarrassing and often irritating habit of pleadings.

With younger children, it is difficult getting them latched on to an idea. After multiple failed attempts, either because of complicated rules, disconnects between Anita and me, monitoring overheads etc., we were on the brink of giving up. However, this last time, we decided to keep it simple with only one goal, to get them addicted to the system and have them experience the joy of earning the things they desired.

With time, the system evolved. What started with baby steps, helped achieve a lot in the long run. Their pride at accomplishing an objective could be sensed for days. Given their age, we were uncomfortable handing out money directly and hence opted for the point system. It was like token money, where each point translated to certain amount in rupees. In addition, it also helped monitor what the kids wanted to buy.

Though simple, the system did wonders! In addition to exposing them to prioritizing, realizing the value of money, decision-making, budgeting etc., it also introduced them to various other concepts. Recollecting an instance where they desired IPods, I remember there being an agreement on this being a good 'want' despite which they would need to earn them. Doing math, they figured the number of points needed to buy the IPods. With a target set, both worked aggressively gathering points. About a month from then, we noticed them losing steam with their enthusiasm fading. The task seemed demanding and no amount of stimuli could kindle their enthusiasm. To lure them, I went ahead with procuring the IPods and demonstrated my disappointment unable to hand it to them. The kids seemed desperate to have them and would do anything to lay their hands on it. I then took the opportunity to introduce them to the concept of leasing. They leased it in exchange of points for 18 months, after which it was theirs for keeps.

Dr. Bhooshan Shukla - Children have difficulty understanding long time perspective. For a 10 year old, having to wait for a year to earn their 'want', is like 10% of their life. It is a huge growth jump, psychologically and physically for the child. Instead, doing something once in few weeks offers lot more value. Even psychologically giving multiple smaller positive feedbacks is better than giving one big positive feedback.

The same system was further used to encourage children to read non-fictional books, watch informative videos, curtail television time, waking early and so on. It further evolved to account for things such as bad behavior, inability to keep commitments etc.

Dr. Bhooshan Shukla - Budgeting is a fundamental and important skill that children need to learn. There can be broad guidelines on where not to spend. Otherwise it is their money and they should have the freedom to do what they want.

Despite its expanse, certain 'wants' were out of bounds. It was not about affordability; it just didn't make sense. One such example was children asking for mobile phones. It was like a can of worms surfacing every time somebody they knew procured one. Regardless of the explanations one doled out, kids had difficulty understanding. They would persist with their negotiation tactics, shooting proposals like what if I got better grades, why should you have a problem if I am buying it using my points etc.

An off-shoot of the system was that we made good negotiators out of our children. Every point, every rule became open grounds for negotiations. Trust started fading and managing the system became a nightmare. What worked well through their toddlers days had to be scrapped with them entering teenage. The collective effort that went into making the system work was greater than its returns.

Dr. Bhooshan Shukla - When children get into the salary or points mode, they become negotiator and ruthless ones at that. It is very difficult to negotiate with them, unless in the short term parents are ready to hurt them, and in the bargain themselves. Some parents are not comfortable, while some seem content. Again, negotiation is a very important skill in life, but is family the place where it should be practiced?

Being liberal with the point system at the start and getting children hooked on to it is a good beginning. Children get hooked when they see the system functioning, implying that their 'wants' are being met. Once hooked, refine ground rules, put penalty clauses, exceptions etc. A system with defined goals makes it easier for children to adopt it. With each goal being met, evolve the system further. For example, where the goal is to encourage reading among children and you notice it being imbibed by your child, it implies time to have a new goal and thus new means of gathering points. It is also important to not have all of the child's 'wants' induced through the system. The whole idea is to make it a winning situation for both, parents and children. Parents thus have a vehicle by which they can provide all the luxuries and children getting the opportunity to earn it.

Owning up to ones actions

*'Your actions are your only true belongings.' ~**Allan Lokos***

While in a profession, one of the things I believed strongly in was giving ownership. From a parenting perspective, I could see two aspects. The first being responsible for the things one owns and the second owning ones actions. Contrary to my belief what I did well, was nurture a joint sense of ownership. While children had ownership, the responsibility often lay with me. What my children really needed was ownership in its true sense.

Ownership with responsibility - To illustrate my point, let me share a personal experience. Rushil, all of four then had a habit of experimenting with his toys making it seem as though the word gentle was not part of his lexicon. His curiosity reached a point where not a single toy of his was in its original state. It was not that he did this in any kind of rage; instead, he did it in a very playful mood. Irrespective of what I said, a new toy faced the same consequence. I started wondering if there was something we were doing to fuel this behavior of his. Then one evening when I was relaxing after dinner, he got a broken toy and asked me to fix it. As usual, I told him that I would fix it on the weekend. It was then that it struck me; I was the probable reason for his rough behavior. There was no doubt that he was the curious kind, but the assurance came from the fact that if a toy broke I was always there to fix it! It probably made him think that breaking and fixing was just a cyclical process.

Dr. Bhooshan Shukla: Ownership for children is about managing their time, resources, and getting in and out of trouble. It is the most important thing to learn. These days, anxiety has come to be such an important component of parenting that unless overcome, children's experiences are going to be limited.

Intent on curbing his behavior, I decided to set some ground rules. In my chat with him, I explained that while buying toys was my responsibility, owning and taking care of them were his. Starting today, he would have to take care of his toys and play carefully. If broken henceforth, I would no longer be fixing them and he would have to continue playing with the broken toy or mend them on his own. Being just four then, it did not seem to matter what I said as he continued playing in his usual style. His toys would break and he would bring them to me. I would remind him about our agreement of not fixing them. A few occasion later, he started approaching his grandparents to fix them whenever they came over. I shared my observation with his grandparents and told them about the agreement. They understood and sided with me. The message was now starting to resonate and he tried fixing them himself. With limited success and lots of broken toys, we started to observe a change. While his exploration continued, he also started taking care of his toys. Now 14, the curiosity in him is still alive and kicking though he has become a lot more responsible, given that he has been earning his toys as in "Earning It".

While he owned the toys, having ownership without responsibility did not yield much in terms of learning. I believe, ownership comes naturally to children though responsibility is a different ball game and this is where I struggled. The thought of my child going through any kind of discomfort somehow did not feel right. By exercising joint ownership, we stepped in every time we sensed failure. This dulled their sense of ownership and thus not only expected us when in trouble but also never learned to own their actions. They seemed to miss out on the lessons failures teach and the fact that making mistakes is human. Giving responsibility along with ownership seems like a package deal.

Along came the freedom to do things their way, and the liberty to make mistakes. In order to ensure a successful hands-off deal, I was

• Required to exhibit patience

• Be accepting of the child's failures/mistakes

• Realize that there is more than one-way of doing things right

There were other instances as well of my reluctance to give them their share of responsibility/freedom. One such place was their bedroom. Done with pride, its decor was guarded closely. While they knew it was their room, they had little freedom to put up posters or wall hangings since it would alter the looks of the room. While one believed in asking for permission the other believed in asking for forgiveness. My preference to get things done in a certain way often implied taking over the reins. With little room to do things there way, all that the children did was focus on execution.

Dr. Bhooshan Shukla - Children need their individualism and if you do not encourage it within the family, they will express it elsewhere. Unable to express it within the family, they feel outcasts and develop a sense of rebellion. Typically, adolescent will put up those horrible posters; like skull and bones on the door, and that should be fine. After a while, they will grow over this childishness and take it off. The good things about kids is whatever you don't like, they will grow over it.

To eliminate a behavioral trait one needs to realize that children are eventual drivers of their lives. Sooner they are on the wheel, more the time parents get to prepare them for their journey. Giving ownership and responsibility is not about whether to give it or not, instead it is about when to give it.

Owning ones actions - Besides ownership, the other important aspect that I believe children ought to be educated about is to own up their actions.

It saddened us to see that a lot of the discipline put in place was not internalized. The kids did it either because of fear or out of respect. The elder one was usually the first to see the merits and my guess is she also needed a break. The younger one preferred learning from experiences, which did not come as a surprise. Though the caring kind we made it difficult for them to own their actions.

Alarmed of being targeted or penalized, our children were apprehensive of owning their action. Instead, they preferred giving it a miss or blaming it on circumstances. Such traits persisted irrespective of the size of the problem. It was quite likely a side-effect of our non-receptive attitude towards their mistakes.

Dr. Yajyoti Singh - Internalizing of discipline is one of the most important aims of parenting. You do not want a child to do a particular thing only because he/she is being watched. You need to get him/her into a system of internalizing where they understand that whatever they do is for themselves and not for others. This is what is expected of me, even if I am not being watched by mom/dad. The final aim of discipline is internalizing.

Considering it a revelation, we were not ready to give up yet. Exploring the topic further lead us to some basic understanding of why the method used were not helping children internalize. Any non-conformity of rules often resulted in punishment and the severity varied depending on the situation and mood. Penalizing not only made it difficult for children to internalize, instead it often left the impression of us being unfair.

Filling in with consequences for penalties, we took another approach. This meant making them aware that consequences were a result of their actions and not penalizing bad behavior. Now it was up-to them to decide on their action. Ensuring easier adoption, we once again relied on compartmentalization of consequences, thus ensuring that boundaries did not get crossed.

If the child missed the daily chores of drying the washed laundries then consequences would mean folding the clothes as well for a week. Overusing the allotted T.V. time would result in a consequence of T.V. becoming available only after all activities for the day were completed. The consequences were not something that we cooked up in random, instead was decided before the incident occurred. In a way, consequences helped children learn to control their behavior.

The other thing that required revisiting was the number of rules. Having rules on every step of the child's way was nothing but a nuisance. Despite our best efforts, we ended up having a handful of them. Those retained were done with the consent of the children.

We continue to wonder if we should have done it earlier. In hindsight, we got the opportunity to learn from our mistakes and also let them loose while still being raised at home.

The Gist

Values at my core played an important role in defining who I am and what matters to me. Youth may not understand the significance of values and may therefore not fully comprehend what they imbibe. For me, recognizing them helped me become consistent and overcome my anxieties of what my actions portrayed.

Being thankful for what one has is applicable not just to the young. I did look for happiness in materialistic pursuits while fully comprehending the difference between needs and wants. Children too are likely to feel deprived irrespective of their demands getting fulfilled. Having a discussion with them was not trivial by any means though they ought to know that not all of their wants will be met.

Providing children with the means to earn their wants was something that worked fine till their teenage. Aside from learning concepts such as prioritizing and decision-making, they also got to learn budgeting and planning. Focus though seems to have been lost for goals that took longer than a couple of months, for which another mechanism was devised. An offshoot of the program was that we made good negotiators out of them. Despite the mixed response, the program was later dropped as the hassle of managing and monitoring it was just not worth the trouble.

Ownership implies two things, being responsible for the things one owns and owning up to one's actions. While children had ownership, the responsibility often lay with us. What was ideally needed was to devolve ownership onto them. They could then express their individuality and have the freedom to make mistakes. Giving them the liberty saddened us in that none of the discipline put in place was internalized. Thankfully, the insight helped us highlight the consequences of their action.

An exercise on 'Relaying Values'

Significance of Values

a) Of all your behaviors, which do you think are inconsistent with your values?

b) Have you attempted to share your values with your family? If so, what are those?

c) Have your spouse and children list down values you give top priority to?

d) According to you, what are the family values your children have inherited from you?

Being thankful for what one has

e) What are the things that make you happy? Are they little things that matter or materialistic pursuits?

f) Do you believe your children are sensitized to the difference between needs and wants?

g) Do you struggle to keep up with your children's ongoing demands?

h) Do you believe in giving things to children even before they ask?

Earning it

i) How do your encourage children to do things outside their routine?

j) Are there programs in place that help children earn their wants?

k) If so, what have been the highlights and drawback of the program?

Owning up to ones actions

l) List those areas wherein you believe children have ownership along with responsibility.

m) How do you ensure your children's internalized discipline?

n) How often do you step in and take control of your child's tasks?

Letting Go

'Letting go off what you love is difficult, but holding on to something that isn't meant for you is impossible.'

It was monsoon and the downpour heavy. With an umbrella and toilet roll in one hand and a leash on the other, I was treading carefully through the waterlogged pathway with our pet dog Simba. Stray by birth, it had the attitude of a Lion and so too a mane. Struggling to align the umbrella, I was furious at Simba for tugging me towards the side. Dragging him back, I saw something flutter. A closer look, revealed a Mynah chick. Drenched and sluggish, it was as though waiting for a feline to put it out of its misery. I quickly grabbed it with the tissue paper, hoping to soak away some of the water.

Getting home, I punched penny-sized holes in a shoe box and placed our feathery guest in it next to a 16 Watt CFL. In about 15 minutes, I could hear movements. Relieved, I continued with Simba's walk. About 20 meters away from where I found the chick, lay another one, a little more active, and bigger.

Unsure if they were related, I went through the same steps to keep it warm. With doubts about finding worms, I force-fed it some soaked green lentils. Worried that ants might get to them, I hung the boxes on the lamp all through the night. Pondering how to nurture them, I devised a plan to hoist the boxes high up on the bedroom window. This would not only keep predators such as crows, kites and cats at bay but also make them accessible to their parents. With the chicks calling out, there was a good chance my plan might work.

With the boxes in place and me hiding behind the bed, I gave myself half an hour, before formulating another plan. In little less than 15 minutes, the Mynah parents and chicks were united. At dusk, I lowered them down and left them to roam free in the bedroom. As a foster parent, this became a routine for the next 7 days. On the 8th day, around noon I noticed the healthy chick perching on top of the box. Anxious the crows might get to it, I tried grabbing it. It flew to a nearby tree and from there on to the neighbor's porch. While I was relieved to see its ability to fly, it seemed rather abrupt and I missed wishing it luck.

Noting its companion's absence, the other chick became more active. When left alone in the bedroom, I noticed that it was attempting to fly and had landing issues. Hoping for some sunshine and its foot to get better, I decided to hold it back for 2 more days. The next day was bright and warm and the chick was not its usual sickly self. Flapping aggressively, it was attempting hard to cut loose. I was in a dilemma. Should I let it go or do I stick to my earlier plan? Sticking to my earlier plan, I prayed that nothing should happen to the chick for another day.

As dusk approached, I shortened my evening walk to check on our feathery friend. Reaching closer to home, Rashi in a moist voice mentioned seeing Phoebe (an adopted stray cat) with a chick in her mouth. For a moment I felt the world pause. Rushing upstairs towards the bedroom window, my heart sank on seeing the mangled box.

I stayed up all night wondering whether the chick was conveying a message. How could I have such bad judgment? Was my sixth sense so bad? In spite of being an avid nature lover, I felt responsible for the chick's loss.

I realized what got me worried was my inability to let go. This got me thinking of how I could prevent it from affecting my children.

Dr. Bhooshan Shukla - Detachment is a key aspect of parenting. Children are biologically trained to be attached to their parents, an evolutionary mechanism built into us for survival. As maturity kicks in at 12 or 13, they start becoming independent, another mechanism to get rid of the attachment.

In the modern world, that detachment does not seem to happen. With children's in their 60s, parents into their 80s, still tell the former how to make a cup of tea. Detachment thus needs to happen.

Children meant the world to me. They were beyond being just the top priority. In fact, if there is the one thing I want to be an ace in life, it is Parenting.

Having too much expectation signifies putting too much pressure. Holding things that close, one thing was certain, I would never be able to let go. Probably nothing would hurt me more than my own failure as a parent.

Constructive Parenting

*'The secret of improving is in parenting.'~ **Immanuel Kant***

Parents, in attempting to be the best, are as stretched as children. Overcoming engagement one after the other, they have little time to pause and evaluate their effectiveness. Effectiveness not in terms of being measured against set standards but just in knowing that whatever they do yields the desired outcome. Thus the question, 'Does "effective" mean working hard or working smart' seems to get evaded.

Hell-bent on making children successful by substituting their childhood spirit with programs, are we making it a pleasurable experience? Burdened with our expectations and suppressed of originality, how successful can they be? How then can we make the journey of parenting enjoyable both for the child as also us?

Enjoying parenting

*'If you have never been hated by your child, you have never been a parent.' ~ **Bette Davis***

Some years ago, the question 'Do you enjoy parenting' would have evoked a response of being on the fence with certain aspects bringing pain and the rest pleasure. Anita would likely have complained of getting clobbered from both, the children and me. Parenting then was like sailing through rough waters where the ride was only occasionally smooth. No two rides can ever be the same. Some gave heartburns while others lead to frustration. That said, after every ride, you feel a sense of accomplishment and looked forward to the next ride.

While the sense of accomplishment came from the vast learning, the heartburns and frustrations were often caused by our views of right or wrong. Me being the exploring kind made things only worse. I saw opportunity in every aspect, resulting in changes far too frequent. I over analyzed and challenged myself to come up with solutions. While I enjoyed the learning, the pressure was felt more by the kids and Anita.

A recourse was more than required to make it a pleasurable experience as also to avoid stressing not just others but ourselves as well. This implied reiterating the following: providing unconditional love, analyzing one's effectiveness, avoiding the tendency to be a super parent and most of all, empathizing with oneself.

Unconditional love - Interestingly how I defined unconditional love turned out to be a reminder of my learning from the prior sections. It meant dropping any preconceived image of that perfect child and accepting them the way they were. I purposely avoided burdening them with my expectations and instead learnt to nurture their uniqueness. Staying confined within role boundaries meant I could avoid getting swayed. Children were assured that irrespective of the method we practice, giving love and affection would always be paramount and nothing would affect that relationship.

Analyzing ones effectiveness - Often our notion of providing the best translates to working hard with little time to pause. Anita was that kind, she hardly took the time to assess the situation and verify if her approaches were constructive. Not taking the time to analyze often meant pushing the same cause. Pushing the same cause again and again can be stressful not just for the parent but also the child. When viewed from a child's perspective, it would seem like dealing with noise. When persisted, children involuntarily filter out such noises giving out the impression of parents being ignored.

Dr. Yajyoti Singh - In order for parents to be effective, knowing where to spend time and how much requires stepping back and analyzing. Doing the same basic routine repeatedly is unlikely to help anybody.

There is no doubt that parenting is hard work, and to make it worse, we push ourselves harder. Doing so brought in other aspects, such as monotony. Should parenting with all its challenges ever feel monotonous? I recollect my cousin preparing three distinct lunches to cater to different tastes every morning, before the family left for the day. She worked her heart out, but it never seemed to reduce her stress. She believed in dealing with a day as it passed. While a long-term solution may seem time consuming to arrive at, the overall effort spent is considerably less as compared to the combined effort put in every day. She thus lacked the time to step back, rethink her approach and implement it.

While some problems need to be broken down to understand better, others need to be magnified. Magnifying helps understand the gravity of the situation and thus the long-term impact of our actions. Though she never complained, the accumulated stress must have vented itself out in some way on her loved ones. The key to avoid stress, which accompanies unrelenting hard work, is to step back, analyze the situation and make required course corrections where it is so desired.

Avoid being a super parent - Having always wanted to be a super-parent, it was difficult accepting my parental limitation. Honestly, we lacked a basic understanding of what we expected of them. Additionally, we did not have any clue of what our priorities were. Wanting them to be better and more successful, we stretched our resources to ensure their upbringing was never compromised. In the absence of a priority list of things that mattered, we attended to everything that caught our eye, be it failing to brush their teeth or their untied shoelaces. Somewhere the realization of not being a superman or superwoman was required. In attending to them all, we were not only being less effective but also creating stress.

Dr. Bhooshan Shukla - Parents struggle knowing their expectation from children. Majority of what one expects from their children is nothing but their own aspirations. We look at the progression of time and generation as an investment which needs to grow at a certain rate. Linear progression is what parents expect but looking around we realize progression in life is nothing but randomness with a bunch of ups and downs.

I often thought what a parent needs is a big picture/roadmap of where the child is headed. A similar thing during my growing years would have made a world of difference. I was so wrong! Parenting with all its expansive responsibility still has its limits. My duty as a parent was to do the best in raising children and leaving the rest to them. Instead, I was so pre-occupied in meeting objectives, that I missed out on their perspective and thus failed in accepting them. Being in their shoes made me realize that quite often they put in their best and all they got in return was my fury. While my efforts and frustration never went unaccounted, theirs were rarely counted. I would hate to be a child who is constantly nagged and picked on for one thing after another.

Self Empathy - Another aspect that we missed was self-empathy. I pushed Anita hoping to extract the most and pressurized myself to do better. It was not until our children's first camp that we realize we did not have a life without them. Inadvertently just like our predecessors, we were also making it our purpose to raise children. It was time for yet another improvement to give ourselves space, in other words personal time; time, which would help in cultivating hobbies or entertaining ourselves.

With the day already packed, finding time felt like pulling a needle from a tightly bunched haystack. Two exercises in particular helped; the first was about ordering our priorities and the other was being able to multi-task. The former helped figure out where we spend most of our time. As for multitasking, identifying activities where one is involved physically are best candidates. The activity that worked best for me, with little distraction was washing my car. Considering this a personal space, where I was in harmony with myself, I did most of my thinking. Most parents are likely to have similar interest such as watering plants, walking, dusting, cooking etc. which make good slots for multitasking.

While we managed to stay positive through it all, there were ample stressful moments. Although parenting is about the child, it was important knowing that a stressed parent can never equate to happy child. Approaches that require lot of Band-Aid and duct tape to hold it all together are probably not worth pushing forward. It is better to revisit and start fresh.

Adding too much value

'Stop adding too much value.' ~ **Marshall Goldsmith**

Both Anita and I were raised in situations where privacy had little meaning. We had developed a natural flair for butting our nose around. In fact, it was so normal, that we did not find it objectionable to ingest ourselves in any conversation that happened around us.

While this behavior can be experienced across topics, let us focus on how it impacts conversations. Interestingly, it is common to notice people having difficulty realizing that not every discussion involves all. For some unknown reason, we feel welcomed to participate, stretch the discussion and affect its closure.

While everybody is entitled to his or her opinion, I wonder why we struggle to keep ourselves out of certain conversations. Wouldn't it be nice, if people shared their opinion only when it matters? Even something as simple as my niece deciding to have a haircut would quickly turn political at home. Suddenly everybody in the family had a say with the poor child getting pressurized from exercising her own will. Did this behavior stem from a certain self-belief in one's being needed?

We fancy ourselves as givers, with the ability to make a difference wherever involved. This belief that deters from trusting and delegating is what I call adding too much value.

Is it because of the fear that things may not happen the way we expect them? A mistake might be made, a wrong decision taken or a rework required. In the big scheme of things, these may be very small incidents, yet we hold them close to our hearts and have difficulty letting go.

Dr. Bhooshan Shukla - What we encounter is that no parents want their children to be normal. They seem disappointed when their children are statistically normal. One needs to realize that nothing exceptional is going to happen in the first 18 years of their life, unless they are gifted sportsperson or artist. Majority of them peak close to their 40s which in a way is better than those who peak in their 20's and struggle to figure out what's next.

Being selective of the discussions one participates in does not mean shutting off; it instead implies choosing to participate in only those where required. Selecting the discussion to participate in also implies trust in others involved and delegating. It is also about giving others the required space and opportunity to do things their way.

Here is a scenario that commonly takes place in our daily lives of a child expressing her unhappiness to her mother over tiffin provided for school.

--------- **Start Conversation** ------------

Jackie : Mom, I do not know what is wrong with you. I have told you so many times that I do not like leafy vegetables. Why then do you keep sending them in the tiffin?

Mother : Leafy vegetable are good for you, you cannot be eating only potatoes.

Jackie : What is wrong with potatoes? Why do you want things done your way? Why can't you for once, just listen?

Father : Jackie you are now crossing limits. Is this how you speak with your mother? Do your friends too speak in a similar fashion?

Father : You have to learn to eat all kinds of vegetables, no further discussion.

--------- **End Conversation** -----------

The above discussion might seem normal in a household. When we encounter family members discussing something, and notice things not going right, we feel the urge to interject and get things in order. This in other words is adding too much value. In the above example, Jackie and her mother are having a discussion and the father seems like the outsider doing so for the sake of the conversation.

Though he is pitching in to add value, he is in reality meddling in and complicating the matter further. In the case of this discussion, the mother is the right person to know if Jackie had crossed her limits. Ideally, the father should have trusted the mother to do the right thing. It is thus quite common for people to barge into discussions without understanding the context and swaying it in another direction. A simple prior understanding of whether one is needed in such situations or not could help. Not wanting to be involved does not imply lack of interest. Instead it implies trust in one's ability to resolve the issue, which, in this case could be with the mother and child. Any observation(s) that the father in the above instance wanted to share either with the mother or the daughter could have taken place in private. Such an arrangement ensures that the discussion stays focused.

Agreements such as these may seem offending to the elderly, however they need to be taken into confidence. Explaining the goals of the arrangement and letting them voice their opinion in private can help in achieving this. The concerned person, a mediator, after having heard everybody's views can take the most appropriate decision. Such arrangements help in quicker resolution of contentious issues and are most likely to benefit children as they are usually the ones at the receiving end what with everybody exercising their authority over them.

Taking a step back and delegating not only provide others with opportunities, but also helps from spreading one-self thin. Spreading thin often dilutes one's stand and ability to make a difference where it matters most. Delegation thus becomes an important aspect of letting go. Delegation works best when done in agreement with the delegate, thus identifying areas each individual will be responsible for. My observation is the older and wiser one gets, the more likelihood of having difficulty in delegating and staying out of conversations.

Dr. Yajyoti Singh - Giving space to the child should not be about convenience. It is important not to give space such that it causes disconnects. While delegating is important, staying engaged is equally important.

Keeping conversations focused help deal with one thing at a time and getting quicker resolution. If you happen to notice people drifting during conversation, it is fair to highlight the same and focus instead on the topic at hand. Focusing on a few and important conversation help us achieve more with fewer communication gaps.

Team - work
'Alone we can do so little; together we can do so much.' ~**Helen Keller**

Back during my children's toddler days, they would unfailingly greet me from work with a recurrent question "Kya Laye?" – What do you have for me? Candies were an implicit. Initially it sounded cute. As encouragement, I would hide candies in my shoulder bag which would be spotted within seconds. In a matter of few weeks, my excitement started to wane, especially on days when I forgot to pick candies from my office desk. The response would then be more of a spontaneous outburst, from 'Why don't you give them candies?' to 'Why do we have to go through this ritual every day?' Anita, furious of their behavior would complain of them having had their daily quota. To keep my position, I would request her to give some. Clearly, our children were capitalizing on the gaps we had left behind and pitting the two of us against each other.

Capitalizing on our inability to work as a team, our children conveniently made soft targets out of us. It meant exploiting gaps and opportunities that existed in terms of our understanding of situations. It included such acts like choosing the dominant amongst the two of us, working on our compassion or our preoccupation, and so on. In short, they used all possible techniques to get their work done. It is as though they were past masters at understanding parents. One such technique was to approach with their asks when we were not exactly in a position to give it a serious thought, like when we were on the phone or had guests at home etc. Where required, they would also override our decision by pitting us against each other causing conflicts.

Dr. Shreeram Geet - Teamwork should be inherent in parents even before the child is born. If not, it is likely to get extended and affect the child. Teamwork in other words means collaborating, one teaches mathematics, the other languages etc. Lack of team effort, implies identifying faults and questioning every aspect in the presence of the child. For e.g. A child taken to the market, may evoke comment from the spouse like, 'why take him to market, is he going to purchase things life-long'. Children learn to take advantage of such situations and real conflicts between parents start.

For us, working as a team was not about choice, instead it was a necessity. Irrespective of our differences, children should have no option but to see us as one united force. Although between the two, we possessed skills that complemented each other, we never cared to leverage them. For children to deal with individual parents can be frustrating especially when parents have difficulty honoring each other's commitments and overrides the other's actions/ decisions. It's like dealing with two sets of contrary commands given at the same time.

I recollect another incident where our children of roughly 10 and 8 years taking advantage and pitting us against each other. My focus during the time, was addressing long-term activities, while Anita's was to focus on day-to-day activities. Taking advantage of my absence, the children would convince their mom and either skip activities such as writing composition or cut short others such as physical activities. Occasionally, they would also present things out of context, fueling conflicts between the two of us. When analyzed, we realized that our children were being natural in exploiting gaps that had been made available by circumstances. What was also evident to them was the lack of buy-into each other's program. While Anita was busy with her set of activities, I was driving my set of initiatives. Appreciating their sense of observation was one thing though and putting an immediate end to it was another.

Reaching a resolution required approaching it in three steps.

Step 1 - The first was never to discuss matters pertaining to children in their presence. While opinions were gathered and debate encouraged, all discussion and arguments were held away from the child.

Step 2 - The second step was to designate areas and give each other some space. In other words, if their mother is the one taking care of their education, then she should be the one making relevant decisions. Since she will be doing the grind, she would be better equipped to know what is required and what is not. This does not mean that the father is not involved; instead, his involvement will be behind the scene. It will be the mother's responsibility to stay in sync with the father as and when required.

Step 3 - The third step was to stay united, respect each other's decision and avoid challenging the latter in the child's presence. For the child, the decision irrespective of the parent would be unanimous. If the child approached a parent for decision beyond their designated area(s), such parent must ask the other what has already been conveyed and apply the same.

The approach was then shared with the children. Highlighting past observations, we emphasized why flouting would be unacceptable. Bringing about a change took time to be accepted and perfected. Children, upon trying their earlier tricks were reminded about the rules to be followed. Surprisingly, on our very next wedding anniversary, we got a card from our daughter highlighting one of the attributes as "Always United". This was proof enough that the system was working!

Dr. Bhooshan Shukla - This is probably one of the most vital things. We have a contrast here. Right from childhood we teach our children to consider every other person around them as their competitor. We actually kill the notion of friendship and cooperation. This continues till the child finishes education, and then suddenly realizes the limitations of not being a good team player. Companies on the other hand pay top money to bring in external trainers and enhance teamwork. You train them one way for 20 to 23 years of their lives and then ask them to turnaround, only because that phase required it! It does not go away that easy. The notion of teamwork should start right in the family. When they see parents cooperating, backing each other without a fight, that is when they learn. They need to see that though people are doing different things, we are one family. What we do has a common sense of purpose, a common direction.

In the process, we learnt that teamwork is not about shedding individual traits and pretending to be one. Instead, it is about building consensus, backing decision and supporting each other's causes. The mantra being, either convince or be convinced. When parents do not work in tandem, children notice and maintain a record in their so-called reputation system. This system is based not on what parents say; instead, it is based on what they do. It not only helps build the parent's credibility, but also helps in knowing the leeway offered, given the situation. Teamwork is about keeping the children from being misled and ensuring that gaps between parents' are not exploited. On all other occasion such as playing with them, spending quality time, sharing common interests etc., parents should continue being their usual self with their distinct personalities intact.

Staying united has its benefits for both children and parent. While parents learn to respect each other's space and viewpoints, children learn the importance of working as a team. Working as a team also applies to grandparents if living under the same roof. With no prior context, they have a tendency of overriding parents' decisions. Staying united is not a choice but a need in keeping families healthy.

The Gist

Letting go might sound easy but in reality, the most difficult to achieve. Making one-self redundant seemed unsatisfying, but seeing other step-up felt gratifying.

A significant change which came about when realization dawned was that regardless of how much pressure we took, children would grow up being whatever suits them best. Instead of getting stressed, we tried creating positive influences and enjoying parenting. This helped us step back, analyze the situation and avoid being a super-parent.

While the section on 'Adding Too Much Value' focuses on conversation, it pretty much applies to every aspect of family life. Whether it is about doing the dishes or drying the clothes, the topic does have its applicability. Our practice has reached a point where interrupting an activity is often discouraged by our children, with a 'will come back to you if need be' response!

In hindsight, I am surprised at how we missed working as a team. Thanks to our children's highlighting the same, it has helped not just work together but has also complemented each other. Children these days rely on our teamwork to share things otherwise deemed uncomfortable to share with us while in our presence.

An exercise on 'Constructive Parenting'

Enjoying parenting

   a)   Which aspect of parenting brings you pleasure?

   b)   Do you prefer pushing the same cause or stepping back and analyzing your approaches' effectiveness?

   c)   Are you stretched in attempting to be a super parent?

   d)   How often do you take the time to rejuvenate yourself?

Adding too much value

   e)   Do you also believe that an activity when delegated to a focused few yields faster resolution?

   f)   Do you expect things be done just as you prefer it?

   g)   How difficult is it for you to let go off things?

Team - work

   h)   Have you experienced children taking advantages of the gaps that exist between you and your spouse?

   i)   How effective are you and your spouse as a team?

   j)   In what aspects do you complement each other?

Empathic Parenting

'The opposite of anger is not calmness, its empathy.' ~ **Mehmet Oz**

Fortunate at having spent time working abroad, the one thing that never went unnoticed was their interaction with children. I believed myself to be as caring as any other parent though I never seemed that gentle.

As kids grew so did expectation. Soon enough, I was expecting them to behave like grown-ups when the child in them was kicking and punching. Making them successful mattered so much that it often accompanied harshness.

What then must be the one key ingredient that matters?

Empathic parenting
'Empathy is about finding echoes of another person in yourself.' ~ **Mohsin Hamid**

The word 'Empathy' was not unknown, nor did I have issues accepting it. However, its application in regards to me was a different matter. On second thoughts, it was probably more about consistency. At work, with friends and in the neighborhood, I was known for my empathy. As a parent, the situations though differed.

Probably driven by anxiety and burdened to make them successful, I expected immediate results. There was no time for song and dance, instead getting quicker resolution mattered most. Being empathic on a few occasions while being critical on the rest often deterred children. When it was required to see the child in them, I saw the individual. When they expected to see the parent in me, what they got was the critic. Being empathic often became a factor of personal judgment.

Taking a leaf from the world of entertainment, there was this video aired on television a long while back. It was about a little girl toppling from a tri-cycle. The dad while recording the video quickly rushes to the crying child asking if she is fine. The sobbing girl lifts her frock, points at her bottom and says 'I got a boo-boo, can you kiss my boo-boo?'. For the little girl, her dad's kiss had the power to do miracles. That is what empathy does, understanding and sharing another person's feeling.

Empathic parenting according to [7]Tamara Parnay is about maintaining a close bond with children. It is about being able to relate to them, sense what they are feeling, help them put their thoughts and feelings into words, and anticipate their reactions. It is about getting down to their level, look lovingly in their eyes, and give them full attention.

My sense of empathy for my children was always a result of my judgment. In some sense it was extreme, they either got my empathy in whole or none of it. I was confusing between 'being practical' and 'being empathic'. Situations where I felt empathy was required to be expressed, I showered them with it. On the rest, I took refuge in being practical.

Claiming to be aware of what was going on in my children's minds empathy was often overlooked for the desire to make them strong and independent.

[7]Tamara Parnay, "Empathic Parenting", http://www.naturalchild.org/guest/tamara_parnay. html (Collected 17 Jul 15)

What they thus got was my ridicule, which unfolded either with 'I told you', or a 'Do you remember what I said', or a 'How many times have I told you', or 'See, you don't listen' etc. I have often risked sounding like a broken record and they did an excellent job deflecting my barbs. Just being there for them and caring was not enough. They needed to see empathy in action not just in thoughts. It was something they expected from me.

In hindsight, I recollect children questioning my contradicting behavior especially with people outside the family. I was not only more patient and tolerant with others but less anxious as well. When it came to my children, I wanted them to mature faster, be responsible and behave like grown-ups.

Children need empathy, and are likely to lean towards those who shoulder it. If not parents, it could very well be grandparents, close family members or neighbors. Lack of empathy towards children also seems to increase their self-pity, which can in turn bring negativity.

Since intentions existed, listening to them and understanding their feeling did not seem exhausting. However, it was easier said than done. Getting them to reveal all of a sudden, required creative questioning without making them feel targeted. At times, the usual old self would erupt requiring discussion to be revisited starting with an apology for my non-empathic behavior. There was no shame, as learning by fire seemed the only way to get rid of the old habit. I was certainly not the kind who in getting involved would miss out on sharing my own feelings. It just required some tweaks and liberal usage of analogies.

There were also those occasions where sensing guilt in my interaction they would expect slackening of rules. In doing so, we realized of them persisting in finding exceptions. It had to be made clear that rules irrespective of the situation had to be followed. The good part was that they were also involved in drafting them and the consequences offered choice. Another aspect that started subsiding was our overindulgence in telling them what they did wrong and what they should be doing instead.

While I am constantly exploring and identifying newer areas of improvement, this probably tops the list. In addition to improving my relation with my children, it is bound to reflect on my parenting style.

Gifting time

*'Time is a created thing. To say 'I don't have time,' is like saying, 'I don't want to.' ~ **Lao Tzu***

To say our world revolved around our offspring must be an understatement, we did nothing without them. Going for a morning walk often involved climbing trees, and returning with both hanging on either of my shoulder, holding tightly the little tufts of hair left on my head. Sleeping time involved different set of activities. Lying on the bed, with the ceiling as a blank canvas, we painted our imaginations. From the Tiger to the Jaguar, we had them all captured. Trembling to the jungle roars, we would all go to sleep. They were not just our source of joy but also our only source of entertainment.

As the kids grew, pastimes changed, family time dwindled and gadget time soared. To make the most of family time, rules had to be ferried in. How we spend time with children could broadly be grouped into three areas, a) time spent in attendance, b) dedicated time and, c) family time.

Anita and I had no confusion between time spent in attendance and dedicated time. Despite her spending most of her time in attending to the children right from serving their morning milk to putting them to bed, she would make it a point to spend some dedicated time; either taking them for a walk or engaging them in games of their liking. Though effort was made to follow a set routine, the focus was always on quality time. Stressed parents are less likely to make the most of such time.

Dr. Yajyoti Singh - I would not quantify dedicated time. I would state that there is no quality time without quantity time. While children need a primary care taker in attendance right from the time they arrive from school who assists them with the likes of homework etc., the same cannot be substituted for dedicated time.

Spending dedicated time was about bonding and connecting at a personal level (knowing their thoughts, viewpoints etc.). It meant creating a channel for them to confide in you, discussing things outside school, opening up to ones' imperfections and breaking the larger-than-life-image. In all it meant investing in trust and staying reminded that 'not quantity but quality matters'.

Identifying a time slot with little or no distraction helps. What clicked was the post-dinner walk. Initially resistant to the idea of breaking their set routine, the children came around to liking it. They came to realize it as their time and enjoyed the attention that came with it. We spoke not just of the past, our childhood and growing up but also shared likes and dislikes, mistakes made, relationships formed, people, priorities etc.

Not all days were the same and occasionally we had to remind ourselves of our role in these one-on-ones. Here we were playing the role of a friend helping establish an unbiased conversation. Whether it was about sharing our childhood adventures or recalling their childhood memories, they enjoyed it all.

There were days when we approached the slots with vested interest, cornering them into discussing activities that occurred during the day. It not only fell flat and worked as a constant reminder that we were in their zone. We steered a conversation away only when we realized they were not up to it. There were the occasional ups and downs with no two days being the same. The healthiest conversations were honest and transparent with little defense even of the spouse. Raised tempers at times did lead to arguments though we stayed true to our goals.

Dr. Yajyoti Singh - Every experience prunes the old synaptic connection. Unless we have new, happy experiences every day, we are not going to be happy people.

Family time seems to be a rarity of late. People are so caught up in their daily rut, including those who run the house, that spending time as a family is often last on their minds. Visit a family in the evening and most likely some member would be glued to the television. With kids' days work getting over only in the evening, the 7 to 9 PM television slot is prime time! Most people including children, given half a chance are likely to stay glued to gadgets including televisions. Dinner times too have moved in the same direction with parents working long hours and children catching up with their favorite shows.

Understandably, family times can never be as exciting as being around gadgets and accessing the digital world. Nevertheless, spending time together as a family is a must. What my family needed was a dedicated slot where we could unwind and create pleasant memories. The slots were blocked well in advance and excuses discouraged. While creativity in picking the slot was encouraged, there was insistence on one rule, that of interaction. Be it casual chats, playing a game of cards, going for a walk or simply browsing through old photographs, interaction was and continues to be a must. Movies were not openly encouraged as they hardly invoked interaction though we still have a blast watching travel programs, treehouse construction and cookery shows.

Till about couple of years ago we spent decent amount of family time over the weekends. The day would start with a walk to the nearby hill rounded off with a game of cricket or badminton in the evening. With time, this changed to going out for breakfasts or lunches over the weekends. Occasionally, we did deviate from this pattern with a reminder to ourselves about the goal of the activity. Lately we have dedicated Saturday evenings for the family with activities such as indoor games, watching old family videos, sharing jokes etc. keeping us occupied.

Time is an invaluable asset; the more it is invested with family, the more returns it brings… in the form of joy! I doubt if my children realize the value of spending time together. At times, they need to be coerced to join us, the outdoors seemingly preferred over indoors. Neither ego nor pride should find room; instead what should is ones' ability to listen and have a heart to heart conversation. Children are unlikely to realize its value till they mature, but an investment it certainly is worth. Though children might be the excuse to implement it, it works equally well with other family members.

Avoid spreading them thin
'A child educated only at school is an uneducated child.' ~ **George Santayana**

Dr. Bhooshan Shukla: Engineering systems are designed for optimization, very unlike biological systems such as humans, which are designed for redundancy. Nature has designed the latter for downtime, survival and happiness and not for ultimate efficiency leading to profitability. Downtime is absolutely necessary and so-called wasting time is one of its best aspects.

Children these days are spread thin through school, sports, music sessions, tuition classes and electronic gadgets. To ensure overall development and focus, we too did our best introducing them to various programs. Keeping them busy not only helped stroke our ego of tapping the genius within them but also ensured their mind were restrained from distractions.

Playtime has been classified as 'structured' and 'unstructured'. Structured playtime have a set objective, where there is a definite start and end, involve rules, or following instructions. Examples of these could be card games, music/dance classes, cricket, football etc. Unstructured playtime means going with the flow, having no rules or objectives. Examples could be playing with a Barbie or a toy car, running around in the park, drawing, painting etc. While structured play can benefit the child in terms of discipline, rules, teamwork, competition, strategy, cooperation etc., unstructured play can bring in social skills, imagination, creativity, independence etc. Thanks to their busy schedules, it's the unstructured playtime that children seem to be missing out on.

Dr. Bhooshan Shukla: Children need down-time and that too non-electronic. Watching television for 2 hours after their art class followed by tennis class, is not downtime. Instead, pottering around the house is. There is enough scientific evidence that over-stimulation damages the brain of young children, particularly with electronic gadgets.

Leave them unchaperoned and one can expect a guaranteed response 'I am getting bored, there is nothing much to do'. It is a little unsettling to know that despite living in an urban setting the kids always need something happening all the time. They seem to have grave difficulty entertaining themselves or being in the companionship of the self. Buried daylong in activities, they are hardly aware of themselves or their surroundings. For them, surrounding seems to play little role in their upbringing, which contributes towards developing their sense of belonging. Today's breed seems more curious and aware of what happens in the world outside than in the place they live. Assured, these children will become successful professionals but wonder if they would grow up to be satisfied humans, without a sense for the surrounding or belonging.

Dr. Yajyoti Singh - Children need free time and this should be regarded as constructive time. Constantly monitored children when left unmonitored, tend to go berserk. It is important for one to be comfortable in ones' own space because one cannot stay busy throughout life.

One Friday evening, Anita & I along with the kids were playing a game of 'Two truths and a lie'. It's a simple game where each participant share three facts that include two truth and a lie. The other participants take turns in identifying the lie. The participant whose lie gets identified the least wins the round. We noticed children struggling to come up with secrets. It is as though there was nothing, but vacuum in their room of secrets. As a child, I recollect tons of memories of times when my parents weren't around. Whether it was stealing guavas from the neighbor's garden or walking barefoot for 15 plus kilometers on the blistering tar road, childhood was all about gathering memories. Unfortunately, my children burdened with our ever-growing expectations seem to have little room to gather memories. It is as if my anxiousness of them grow into an ordinary person was percolating to them.

The external pressures of ever changing landscape, fast paced lifestyle and constantly evolving technology are difficult for grown-ups to get a grasp of let alone children. We had not only enforced back-to-back sessions but pushed them hard on education as well. I recollect stretching Rushil. Unconvinced that the school could do justice while dealing with a student of creative aptitude, I started to overlook his 7th grade study. The goal was to understand the root cause, address them and develop interest in education. In the process, I got so focused on achieving milestones that it did not occur to me that I was causing more harm than good. When exams approached, he seemed more relaxed than usual and spent more time playing than preparing. He was sending out a loud message, and I was not getting it. I was conveniently construing one of his strengths to be his weakness. It was definitely his strength to remain calm, even under pressure. In my attempts to keep him in front of the race, I was endorsing and giving into this undue pressure, which was neither encouraging nor helping the cause.

Probably under pressure to perform, their liking of the structured activities kept wavering. One day, it was about learning karate, which shifted to cricket followed by the urge to participate in a robotics camp.

Unsure if by keeping them on the trot, were we discouraging them from being themselves. Was it also the source of their constant need for change in activities? Upon probing the consistent response was 'it is not fun anymore', the definition of fun varying between 'not learning much' to 'too much involvement'. It became concerning as the activities along with time also called for monetary investments with none being pursued to any logical conclusion. The mischievous mind would also play games and make you wonder if 'lack of fun' was nothing but an excuse for not pushing oneself.

Even after our conscious attempts to give children much needed free time, they continued with their streak for exploring activities. To ensure genuine interest, we devised a plan which made them partners in the initial investment (s). They did it either through their points or their pocket money. With time, this reduced their demand for joining programs.

Dr. Shreeram Geet - Free time is very essential and is what brings in the change. I go by the old dictum 'Change is the spice of life'. Unless there is change, everything becomes stale and boring. Even the school timetables have changes built in to make it easy on children by having short and long breaks.

Being a believer of my role in bringing out the best in the children, I have realized it's pointless achieving the same without making them aware of themselves and the surroundings. For this, they need room to develop their dreams, spend time away from studies, Internet and TV, be in the lap of nature, play and fight with siblings and generally experiment with their surroundings. They need to develop a sense of belonging by way of gathering memories and experiencing life in all its shades on their own. The last calls for meeting people and situations that help them create their own identity. I would rather they make mistakes when we are around to coach and guide them than otherwise.

Dr. Bhooshan Shukla - When parents crave for time, they go on vacations to sit by the sea or over the mountain doing nothing. When the child has a vacation at home, without spending a dime, why should parents object?

Self belief

'My father gave me the greatest gift anyone could give another person, he believed in me.' ~ **Jim Valvano**

On Dad's passing away, Mom's insistence on post funeral rituals was difficult to fathom. More so, given that he believed in god though not in rituals. Mom on the other hand is a firm believer and rituals form an important part of her belief. It is where she gathers her energy, her can-do attitude and the courage to overcome miseries and misfortunes. Self-belief can be described as the confidence one has in the ability to achieve an outcome. People's self-beliefs also have a lot to do with their beliefs; in my mom's case, it was her religious belief. For a large part of my life, I missed this connection.

Like all individuals, my children's self-belief played a significant role in how they perceived things. As a parent, often the first indication of their self-belief was through its symptoms. These symptoms as observed by me were revealed as either being confident, over confident or under confident. As a parent, I have contributed towards all three of them. When their self-belief ebbed, my pep talk has often recharged them. Conversely when it ran high, I often slowed them down and asked them to be realistic. When situations were unmanageable, I have also provoked them with my taunts. A lack of understanding of the topic and how to nurture it in them must have certainly dampened some of their spirits.

Both my children have exhibited different levels of confidence. One is a natural when it comes to activities and can freely jump without a care into any situation. At age 4, he had no issues riding a 500kg thoroughbred single handedly. The first time he saw a swimming pool, he just jumped into it and to everybody's surprise was doggy-paddling around! He took to skates like fish to water. Self-learner of sort, trying to coach him is a challenge. Neither methodical, nor the competitive kind, what he enjoys is the thrill. Lacking knowledge of how he perceived things, and given the head start he extracted, we invariably expected him to do better. Numerous comments and taunts were hurled at him before we realized our mistake of denting his self-belief.

The other one, is not naturally outgoing but an excellent learner, who starts slow and gallops before you know. While her tough outlook can easily win any argument, she is easy to loose track without an instruction manual. We would constantly advise her to be gentle and warm with family or friends though her behavior has hardly changed. Never the one to nurture multiple faces, her consistency and honesty now appear to be her strengths. Retracting our earliest stand, we dropped our attempts at having her develop a facade and encouraged her to be who she was.

The key to nurturing children's self-belief is in sorts revisiting some the sections discussed in the prior chapters.

- **Acceptance** - Accepting children the way they are and realizing their uniqueness creates a sense of belonging in them. For one to feel confident, it is important to feel wanted.

- **Owning up to ones actions** - For children to feel responsible, they need to have the freedom to make decisions and own its consequences.

- **Staying positive** - It is important to find appreciation, even in the most distressing of situations. Learning to focus on the positives comes from practice and practice comes from repeated exposure.

- **Overcoming fear of failure** - Children need encouragement to realize that failures are nothing but 'Another opportunity to learn'. It is important to drive-in the point that failure is not the end; instead it is just a milestone that takes one a step closer to the goal.

My experience tells me that children come with abundance of self-belief which in most cases if not all gets eroded by the parents' lack of trust. Eroding ones self-belief is easy; all that one has to do is raise simple doubts with suspicion and that should do the trick. Instilling it back requires lot more effort, not just from others but from the individual as well. Anxious parents can find motivation in knowing how far they have come instead of getting dejected worrying about how they need to go.

Teenage is about exploration and taking on the world which can make one impulsive. Ideas and perspectives are accepted or rejected basis one's line of thought. Risking over-confidence, they tend to see only their side. Acknowledging their self-belief and expressing trust while making them account for other aspects has not been easy. While unwelcome, somebody has to do it.

Often what we nurture is like a double-edged sword. One such things that we nurtured in our children was independence. With them expressing their individuality, we i.e., parents need to be constantly reminded that this is exactly how we wanted to raise them. Rather than blaming it as a side effect of their growing years, it was important realizing as something that we nurtured over the years.

The Gist

I considered myself a caring and loving parent. Yet, there were some basic ingredients missing, which were vital for a parent-child relationship. One such ingredient was 'Empathy', the area that probably needed the most improvement. Just being a caring and providing parent was not enough. Children also have certain expectation from parents and one of them is being empathic, which my children sorely missed.

With young children, all our time was theirs. As they grew, boundaries started getting defined and special efforts had to be made to ensure we spent time as a family. Like us, children too have their inner circle and the only way to penetrate it is by spending time with them. They are unlikely to see value in spending time as a family until they grow to a certain age; nevertheless this is a worthwhile investment.

A firm believer of the idea of keeping children productive, having free time was never considered constructive. With little time to entertain themselves, they always needed assistance in the form of companionship or gadgets. Smitten by the habit, they continued hopping programs trying to find their niche. With little free time, we hindered not only in developing their sense of belonging to the surroundings but also limited them from gathering memories.

It took me a good part of my career to understand how I was different. The key to my self-belief was self-awareness. Once that started going, things started to piece together. Children carry abundance of hope and self-belief. All I had to do was not chip them away and instead, encourage them to be themselves.

An exercise on 'Empathic Parenting'

Empathic parenting

a) How often do you attempt understanding your child's feeling?

b) How often do you overindulge and have them do things as per your preference?

c) Do their disciplinary actions offer choices?

d) Are children involved in drafting rules that affect them?

e) Which field of activity according to you tops your list of probable improvements?

Gifting time

f) Does your world revolve around your children?

g) Do you take the time to nurture your hobbies or are the children your only source of entertainment?

h) How else do you spend time as a family? Does it involve interaction?

i) How do you differentiate between attending to the child and spending dedicated time?

Avoid spreading them thin

j) Do you ensure that your children are always busy?

k) Do your children have difficulty entertaining themselves?

l) Do your children jump from one program to another?

Self belief

m) What percentage of your comments are sources of encouragement to your children?

n) Have you attempted to understand the nurturing of a child's self belief?

Summing It Up

*'Every child is unique therefore their education should
also be.' ~ Jeannie Fulbright*

Parenting is a never-ending endeavor and there couldn't be a better way to learn it than from our parents. My matriarch of 70 continues treating me like a toddler and I must have argued with her on innumerable occasions on this. It is only of late that I realize her actions are driven by a strong sense of purpose to be of use to her children, the same that has relentlessly driven millions of parents.

I love my children more than anything in the world and trust me when I say they are my top priority. None-the-less, I sure do not want them to be my sole purpose in life. I believe parenting should never be an obligation; no account keeping, no expectation, nothing…. only pure enjoyment deep inside while gathering memories and embracing the learning that comes with it.

I always imagined myself being evaluated against a parenting scorecard. Whether it was teaching cricket or just having fun, I was being internally evaluated. Most often children paid the price with the fun element compromised. While it brought along anxiety, what kept me going was the learning. It was only when I took a break from work and started analyzing the big picture that I realized getting it all wrong.

Visualizing the big picture, made me aware that some of the things I did had little meaning more so when seen in life's entirety. If my goal is to raise happy individuals who are able to connect with themselves and their surroundings, then issues such as excelling in education, being focused, keeping them busy etc. hardly matter. Can I or anybody else take credit for what they become in life? It is like a gardener taking credit for fruits the tree bears. The gardener must have tended to it, shaped it but the gardener did not create the sapling. In other words, a gardener cannot take an apple tree and have it bear mangoes. In the same way, I cannot take a child and make him/her who he/she is not. All I can do is nurture and guide them, ensuring that in the process they do not get conditioned and grow up to be individuals who they are not.

We seem to have an in-built compass that guides us. Some get their direction right early in life, others late. It was difficult comprehending the fact that my children were destined to succeed on their own terms and as per their circumstances. Over the years, one example that describes this observation is that of a diamond nested in each of us. It shines with all its brilliance only when the individual decides to polish it. Others' doing make no difference to the diamond. Anxieties, profound or profane are likely to do only one thing-condition the child's thoughts such that it causes more harm in the long run. Accepting the child, being empathic and making them aware of themselves may probably create a more positive influence.

Like my parents, family and neighbors, I too practiced instinct-based parenting, apparent successful examples of which seem to abound around us. Raising children seem to come naturally to parents and most do it fairly well. A few years ago though, all these thoughts changed when I realized the importance of being content with oneself. Before the realization crept in, I would lay claims to giving children the freedom to be what they want, but with strings attached. I could attempt everything morally within my powers to ensure that my children became a Doctor or an Engineer, i.e., professions which embody "Achievement" to the world. These same thoughts now give me the jitters. I was not just conditioning them to a particular line of thinking but also helping define their definition of success. With such a wrong foundation, how would they ever build their dreams?

My thoughts are often in conflict with those of the prior generation(s) with respect to parenting styles. Goals back then were different, with more emphasis on children's education and establishing them- an arduous task no doubt. While these may have been in order for the previous generation(s), the same may not hold for the current lot. . To establish one's parenting goals today, one needs to ask of themselves what they would like their children to remember them for. The legacy one intends to leave behind is likely to steer their parenting style.

One could argue that most parents with their hands full just raising children and could well do without a diverting predicament in the form of realizing child's true potential. There ought to be a realization that this is not about parents working harder or making the child work harder. Instead, it is about having them become aware of themselves. This, from a parenting standpoint can be summarized into three key elements pertaining to the parent and child. For parents, it is about

Watching ones action	-	This in essence, is about viewing one's actions as reflected by the child's behavior
Being the coach	-	What today's children need is a coach who can nurture their individuality and provide them with much-needed exposure.
Letting go	-	One cannot have it all; better invest where it matters and let go off the rest

As for the child, the three things that will help them differentiate are

Nurturing their individuality	-	Accepting them the way they are and nurturing their uniqueness
Making them self aware	-	Helping them identify the ingredients of their recipe
Being Independent	-	Lending them a free hand to cultivate a sense of ownership

Fortunately parenting does not require lots of training or tools. All that it needs is willingness and an open mind. We, the current crop of parents have an opportunity to turn a new leaf in parenting, taking it further and adopting methods that reflect the needs and aspirations of the newer generation. While at work, I often persuaded people asking 'How much time do you spend planning vacations?' followed by 'How much time do you spend planning your career?' Based on your priorities, are your actions justified? If not, it is time to bring about a change. The same persuasion applies to parenting as well. If your actions are not aligned with your priorities, either your priorities need reshuffling or your actions need realignment.

As parents, we may want the world for our child though none of that could matter. What could is what your child wants for him/ herself. Our job as parents is to be there for them and do the best. When it is time to reflect on the past, one should feel proud for having given it their best shot.

This book is not about making parents feel guilty or inferior in any way. Instead, it is about sharing one's thoughts and tickling ones' brains. It is a testimony to the mistakes I have made as a parent where each mistake has ushered my journey to better parenthood. At times, I have over-reacted and cornered them, at others underprepared and stretched them with occasional doses of leniency in between. This pushing and stretching has helped in continuously understanding my children. These mistakes are like scars that army men carry from conflicts faced. Filled with memories, they will be cherished throughout my life.

Parents have got to believe in themselves and that their abilities are best suited to understand their children. While it is true that no parent would ever let go a wonderful opportunity to make a difference in their child's future, parents should never feel pressurized either because the book recommends something or because other parents in similar situations do things differently. Every child is unique and there is no better a judge than parents.

Do not underestimate you child. A future president, prime minister, social worker, scientist or wild life expert etc. lies hidden therein. The greatest gift parents can ever give their child is by being empathic and making the latter self-aware. Children have to live their life's purpose. Our goal as parents is to guide them towards achieving this in a manner enjoyable to both the child and the parent.

I never thought writing this book could be so enjoyable! It not only assisted me in connecting the dots but also helped me observe and judge my actions. I hope you find it just as enjoyable reading it.

Bibliography

Jacob Sokol, "What You Need to Live a Life of Purpose", http://tinybuddha. com/blog/what-you-need-to-live-a-life-of-purpose/ (collected 18th Feb 2015)

Tarini Peshawaria, " Docs worried about rising teen pregnancy, self-abortion in Gurgaon", http://timesofindia.indiatimes.com/life-style/people/ Docs-worried-about-rising-teen-pregnancy-self-abortion-in-Gurgaon/ articleshow/21274442.cms

Tamara Parnay, "Empathic Parenting", http://www.naturalchild.org/guest/ tamara_parnay.html (collected 17th July 2015)

Jan Hunt, "Importance of Empathic Parenting", http://www.naturalchild. org/jan_hunt/empathic.html (collected 17th July 2015)

http://www.brainyquote.com

Juan Carlos Jimenez, "Types of values", http://significanceofvalues.com/

Elizabeth Nixon and Ann Marie Halpenny, "Perspectives on Parenting Styles and Discipline", http://www.dcya.gov.ie/

Loris Malaguzzi, "Your Image of the Child: Where Teaching Begins", https:// reggioalliance.org/downloads/malaguzzi:ccie:1994.pdf (collected 10th Nov 2015)

James Lehman, "Your Child Is Not Your 'Friend'", http://www. empoweringparents.com/Your-Child-is-not-Your-Friend.php (collected 8th Oct 15)

Debbie Pincus, "Punishments vs. Consequences: Which Are You Using?", http://www.empoweringparents.com/punishments-vs-consequences-which-are-you-using.php (collected 27 Nov 2015)

Dr. Thomas Gordon, "The Power of The Language of Acceptance", http://www.gordontraining.com/ (collected 3 Dec 2015)

"Sense of Purpose", http://www.handsonscotland.co.uk/flourishing_and_wellbeing_in_children_and_young_people/flourishing_topic_frameset.htm (collected 17 Dec 2015)

www.ingramcontent.com/pod-product-compliance
Lightning Source LLC
Chambersburg PA
CBHW031313280626
47169CB00018B/1256